THE NAKED STORM

THE NAKED STORM

C.M. KORNBLUTH

Originally published under the pseudonym "Simon Eisner."

WILDSIDE PRESS

Originally published in 1952.

Published by Wildside Press LLC.
www.wildsidebooks.com

CHAPTER I

PASSENGER BOYCE

Boyce's wife, lying in the exact center of her Hollywood bed, said faintly: "Please, darling, no. I have a headache." All the accessories of a headache were neatly arranged on the blonde wood end table: the squat little bottle of aspirin-phenobarb-codein tablets, the glass of water, the box of cleansing tissues, the bottle of pink capsules, the murder mystery by an Englishwoman. Faced by such corroborative evidence, Boyce could hardly call her a liar.

"After all," he said steadily, "I'm going to Frisco in the morning."

A small twinge passed across her face. "You ought to get a good night's sleep," she said. "You know you never sleep in trains."

He looked down at her. For all the good it did him, Peggy was still a good-looking woman. It was, if anything, too warm in the apartment. But as he looked she drew her pink bed-jacket more snugly over her shoulders.

"What have you got that thing on for?" he demanded. "This isn't a hospital. This is home and I'm your husband."

"Please, darling," she said faintly. "I simply can't argue."

"You and your goddamned headaches," he said.

It startled her, and she was startled even more when he struggled into his overcoat and slammed out of the apartment.

Boyce stood shivering in front of the apartment house under the icy blast from Lake Michigan, wondering angrily what to do next. He was going to San Francisco in the morning and he should get a good night's sleep.

But he was sore.

And a taxi pulled up and the driver's red face pressed against the right front window and stared at him contemptuously as if to say: "Don't just stand there, mister. Get in. That's what I'm here for."

Boyce got in and told the driver: "The Loop. Anywhere in the Loop." Have a drink, he thought, calm down, come back and go to bed. Alone.

It was a fifteen-minute drive from the North Side apartment house to the crowded heart of Chicago. The driver pulled to the curb at State and Van Buren and growled: "One seventy-five."

The face of the meter was set into leather padding at the front of the passenger compartment, below eye-level and badly lit. It might have said anything from thirty-five cents to fifty dollars. Boyce thought briefly of checking the reading, gave up the idea as the beefy face scowled at him, and handed over two singles.

"Thanks," the driver said, taking a two-bit tip for granted and roaring the motor impatiently as he waited for his fare to get out.

Boyce got out and stood a little forlornly on the curb, jostled by late shoppers, newsstand helpers getting out the morning editions, and movie-goers. It was eight o'clock of a January evening. The sheet-iron Christmas trees with which lamp posts in front of the State Street department stores were decorated this year were still up. Sheet-iron discs, brightly painted, swung from the sheet-iron branches. Every once in a while a gust from the lake four blocks to the east caught one of the discs and made it spin wildly and utter a weird banshee wail.

A bright marquee behind him blinked RESTAURANT-BAR and snatches of music, drum and piano, blasted out when its heavy glass doors opened to let patrons in and out. Have one now, Boyce thought, then grab a cab back to the apartment. He ducked into the place, crossing the line between the icy street with its banshee wailing and the warmly noisy inside.

The bar was a U-shaped affair enclosing a platform on which a three-piece combo of flat-faced little brown men were strumming La Cucaracha. Boyce sipped his drink, looking straight ahead except for an occasional furtive glance at the musicians.

Quite a nice place, he thought. Nicer than the too-hot apartment with the too-cold wife. Peggy would ask him where he'd been and he'd simply tell her a Loop nightclub and she'd be burned up but wouldn't give him the satisfaction of letting him know—as if she had any secrets from him!

Served her right. Husband going away in mid-winter and he doesn't even get a look at her, much less a night in bed. That damned bed-jacket.

"Yes, sir!" the barman was saying heartily. "The same?"

Boyce nodded and put a five on the bar. This was adding up already. He reached in a sudden panic for his breast pocket and relaxed when he felt the ticket and reservation. Golden Gate Express, leaves Union Station 9:05 A.M., time for a good breakfast, Car 15, Berth 24U. Always an upper until you got to be Senior Buyer and then the sky was the limit if you weren't too old and if nobody on the Board had a loose-end nephew or cousin to sneak your job away from you. It had happened—not so much in Floor Coverings because you had to know the field from the ground up. But in Furniture and in Appliances the axe could fall on anybody. In Furniture you didn't have to know anything except the way to the Merchandise Mart, where salesmen showed you around and you simply made the best deal you could and that was that. Appliances was easier yet. The appliance men came around and begged you to buy. Floor Coverings, for some reason, was still an old-fashioned business and you had to know who was who, who was honest, who was prompt. And rugs fluctuated wildly with the price of wool. For that kind of buying you needed brains and foresight—

When in God's name was Mr. Oberholtzer going to die or retire? Then Mr. Reiner would move up from Assistant to Buyer and Boyce would move up from Senior Salesman to Assistant and everybody would be happy including Mr. Oberholtzer. Mr. Oberholtzer professed to hate the Store and all its works and yet for five years since his stroke he had been dragging himself to the office to put in a couple of hours and then snooze away the rest of the day. And Reiner did Mr. Oberholtzer's work and Boyce did Reiner's work and there was nobody to keep an eye on the floor force, which was addicted to promising impossible delivery dates and impossible sizes and shades and impossibly low fitting estimates to clinch their sales and commissions.

He said to the waiting bartender: "Wonder if you ever thought of the rug-man's problems?"

"Can't say I have," the meaty man in the white jacket admitted. "The same?"

He was a son of a bitch, too. All they wanted was your money. "No more," Boyce told him. He spun around on his stool and went out into the icy air. He felt fine, and magically there was a taxi waiting for him with the door open.

He climbed in and should have said: "North on the Drive," which would take him home to the headache and the prim bed-jacket. Instead he paused.

"Where to, mister?" the driver finally asked with exaggerated courtesy.

Boyce took the plunge and asked, too casually: "What's a good place to go and kill some time?"

The driver clicked down the meter flag half-way to "waiting" and scratched his chin. "Well, there's the Spanish Casino—"

Boyce recoiled. You could conceivably go there with your wife, but if you went alone and somebody saw you it didn't look too good, what with the percentage girls crawling all over you. He'd heard about it from bachelors on the floor force. Regretfully he said: "Not for me."

The driver didn't mind. "You want to see girls," he said, "there's a rub-joint out west, Castle Gardens."

Boyce was vaguely aware that a rub-joint was a low-down dance hall. "Swell," he said. "Let's go." The driver clicked the flag all the way down and headed west on Van Buren Street.

The river, the big ghostly-white railroad stations, the dark used machine-tool district, the honky-tonks glaring and winking—

Half a dozen times Boyce wanted to tell the driver to head north for his home, but was too shy to change his mind in public. I'm a louse, he thought miserably each time. If she's got a headache she's got a headache. And she doesn't get much fun out of it anyway. I ought to tell this guy to head north. But he didn't.

Castle Gardens was from the outside the windows of the second floor of a corner taxpayer building. You reached the second floor by a flight of creaky stairs. Posters flanked the door: Twenty Beautiful Instructresses, See the Beautiful Palm Room, Admission Free. Cut-out pictures of Esquire girls were pasted on the posters. I'll just go in and see what it's all about, Boyce thought. Admission Free.

When he went through the door at the head of the stairs it was all gloom, heat and noise. Bing Crosby assaulted the ears, louder than any juke-box should be, a faceted mirror ball turned slowly in the center of the ceiling casting blots of light that crawled like insects, and women stood about in metallic evening gowns.

"Check your hat and coat," sounded in his left ear, and a pair of heavy hands started to help him out of the overcoat. Boyce had the feeling that he was being processed like a hog at the stockyards. The owner of the hands and voice, a huge man in a waiter's tux, pressed a disk into his palm. "The check. How many tickets you want?"

"Ten," he said. That should be a dollar.

The big man pulled an accordion of tickets from his pocket, tore off ten and said: "That'll be ten dollars."

"Oh," Boyce said, "I'm sorry. I thought they were cheaper. Can I just have one?"

"Look, mister," said the big man. "You asked for ten, I tore off ten. We have to keep track of the numbers. What's the idea of coming in here without any money?"

"But I have the money—" Boyce said, and realized he was sunk. He took a ten from his wallet, looking carefully at it in the gloom, and handed it over and got his tickets. He tried to read one, but the woman in evening dress bore down on him purposefully.

There was a kind of etiquette. They kept their distance and tried him one at a time. Vague faces asked him in turn, as thighs pressed him: "Dance, honey? Sit in a booth and play around a little? Have some fun?"

He said to a blonde who draped herself over him: "All right. Let's dance."

"You want to give me my tickets first, honey? It's two for a dance."

Clipped again. He tore off two tickets and handed them to her. She hoisted her skirt and tucked them into a stocking top, smiling at him with a face that might have been 16 or 46 in the gloom. But her limbs were firm. "You can do that with the next tickets, honey," she said.

Boyce preened a little. It was turning into quite an evening.

Somebody restarted the thunderous Bing Crosby record and the blonde said: "Let's dance back there where it's nice and dark, honey. My name's Jerrie. What's yours?"

"Sam," he said, following her across the floor. He was a fair dancer, he thought. She'd be pleasantly surprised. They probably got nothing but low-class mutts stepping all over their feet in these places...

He found out where it was nice and dark that dancing in Castle Gardens had very little to do with the feet, and that "rub-joint" was a vividly accurate phrase. Bing Crosby broke off with a squawk about half-way through the record.

"Having fun, Sam?" she asked with a professional low-lidded smile. "You want to hide my tickets for me?" She lifted the hem of her skirt. Unsteadily he tore off two more tickets. She leaned against his hand as he slid them under the top of her stocking. Bing Crosby began to thunder at them again and he straightened quickly and took her in his arms, not wanting to miss one expensive, rewarding note of the dance.

She suggested the Palm Room and "some real fun" after the dance. The big man in the waiter's tux materialized at the curtain behind which the Palm Room lay to collect five dollars cover charge. Boyce gave him a bill and the curtain was drawn on a smaller, even darker room furnished with half a dozen booths, all empty.

"You first, honey," she said, and he slid into a booth. She followed, intimately. "Honey," she said, "how about a couple of tickets for sitting this one out with you?" She sat waiting. Dry-mouthed, Boyce raised her skirt almost furtively and put them with the others.

The big man was back. "What'll it be, Jerrie?" he asked.

"Blue Moon. What are you going to drink, Sam?"

"Rye-gingerale."

She crooned the Bing Crosby song, with dirty lyrics, into his ear and massaged him while they were waiting for their drinks.

"That'll be three dollars," the big man said, putting down a tray with a cocktail and a setup. Jerrie drank her cocktail off in a gulp while Boyce was finding out that he had no more ones, fives or tens. He reluctantly lay a twenty on the table.

"Twenty," announced the big man, virtuously, holding it up. "Be right back."

Boyce poured down his rye-gingerale and Jerrie asked for two more tickets. He gave them to her, and a good workout with them. The waiter returned with a tray on which were four Blue Moons and four rye-gingerales.

"Where's my change?" Boyce asked, astounded.

The big man clunked the tray down on the table and said: "Did you come in here to drink or didn't you? There's your change, mister."

Jerrie massaged him feverishly, saying: "Now honey, don't make a scene just when we were getting along so good. You want to give me a couple of tickets, honey?"

He drained one of the drinks while she gulped two of hers in quick succession, and gave her the tickets. She squealed and pretended he was hurting her and they both laughed heartily and finished their drinks, exchanging caresses.

"Honey," she said, breaking away, "you want to buy some more tickets? Just call Charlie and he'll sell them to you."

"Hell," said Boyce suddenly. "Look, isn't there some place we can go? You got a place? Or a hotel?"

"Don't you like me right here?" Jerrie asked, with mock-surprise. "All it takes is a couple of tickets. I'll call Charlie—"

"Nah," Boyce said. "Don't call Charlie. We c'd get a nice hotel room."

"Honey, how much you got on you tonight?"

"Forty bucks left."

"Look, honey, I'll call Charlie and you buy some tickets and we'll have a couple of drinks and then I'll take you to my place and we'll have a real party on me, honey, how's that?"

"You won't do it for forty bucks?"

Her busy hands took themselves off him and she said in a voice that was suddenly dry and cool: "Act your age, buster. Three-fifty for the hotel, one-fifty for miscellanies, two bucks for the cab, I get what's left and I miss the rush hour here. You want to be a businessman, stick to your own business. Don't try to run mine. Are you going to buy some tickets or aren't you? This is liberty night and we'll be getting the radar trainees from Great Lakes any minute, so make up your mind."

"You goddamned tramp," he said softly. "You remind me of my wife."

Her painted mouth made a surprised scarlet O in the gloom.

"Let me out," he said. She slid from the booth and primly straightened her dress. He ignored her, stalking from the Palm Room unsteadily. A couple of the other women headed his way but he outdistanced them.

"M' hat and coat," he said to the big man, who was standing by the door.

"The check, mister," the big man said patiently. He found it and the man got his hat and coat. "That'll be one dollar, mister," the big man said, not handing them over. Boyce scooped out his change pocket and found four quarters. He got his coat and the big man said: "Come again, mister. Any time. You want to see a real strip show tonight? Private house? Nice mulatto girls? I can give you a card—"

Boyce raced down the creaking stairs and stood in the street breathing big lungfuls of the icy air. Four very young sailors in pea jackets were coming down the street, looking dubiously at house numbers. One of them said: "Hey, heah's the place. Is it aneh good, misteh?"

"'s okay," Boyce mumbled, swaying a little, and they exchanged grins.

"Take it easy, pappy," they told him and went charging up the stairs.

"Suckers," he said viciously, half-aloud, and went on down the street to a glow that promised to be a street of shops where he might pick up a taxi for home. "Suckers." All of us. You can't buy what you want and if your luck's bad you can't marry it either. Her and her goddam headaches. That semi-whore and her goddam tickets. Always something. He knew he couldn't run away from it, but he wished desperately that it was already 9:05 tomorrow morning and that the streamliner was sliding out of Union Station with him aboard. You couldn't run away from it, but you could try.

CHAPTER II

BYSTANDERS

I

The wolf was gaunt and shabby; he slunk cringing through the snow, quailing at every blast of wind. He was starving. His ribs showed plainly and his belly drew up tight; he looked grotesquely like the caricature of a greyhound on the buses. He had eaten last a week ago, a sheep cut out from a Colorado rancher's flock and pulled down running. He had gorged on the sheep and awakened from the heavy sleep to find the bones picked by buzzards. The snow had started about then.

He stopped as a familiar, frightening smell permeated the air. It was the complex smell of man and his works. Oil. Gasoline. Cloth. Fire. Whenever that smell had filled the air before it had been followed by loud, inexplicable noises, rushing things moving faster than he could, stones that did not stay in place as stones should but hurtled through the air and thumped him in the ribs or on the nose. As a cub he had learned about that complex smell; it meant trouble and he had stayed away from it.

But he was starving, and part of the complex smell was meat.

With his hackles up and his heart pounding, he inched toward it through the snow. The smell came from a bundle on the ground, and the bundle did not move. His lips drew back as a strain of polecat and another of mink wafted his way. But the bundle did not move, and it smelled also of meat. His caution was consumed by the raging pain in his belly. He leaped on the bundle and tore at it, worrying away strange layers of pelt and cloth. It did not move; it was frozen. He knew what to do with frozen game. He went for the belly with his long, pointed eyeteeth and opened it up. The exposed organs steamed a little in the icy air.

The wolf crouched down and looked about, growling his ownership. There was nobody to dispute it so he began to gnaw at the liver.

He would live through the winter after all.

II

The three men in the hotel room jumped to their feet as the door slammed open.

"Police," a tall man in the doorway announced. Uniformed patrolmen moved around him and began to search the room, picking up papers, briefcases, opening drawers and closets.

The oldest of the three men, bald, wearing a richly conservative brown suit, said: "I suppose you have a warrant."

"Two of them. Search and arrest. Put on your coats and let's go."

The man in the brown suit took a heavy overcoat from a closet and began to wind a muffler around his neck. He asked almost casually: "What's the charge?"

"Conspiracy to violate gambling laws. Let's go."

"May I phone a lawyer?"

"From the station house. Come on."

One of the uniformed men, a sergeant, was carefully removing something bulky from the rear of a high closet shelf. It was a tape recorder, and its reels were still turning. The man in the brown suit raised his eyebrows. He and another of the room's original occupants looked at the third man. He told the third man sadly: "You think you can get away with such goings-on? I'm surprised at you."

The police lieutenant, admitting nothing, nevertheless gave the third man a chin-up glance. Everybody in the room, however, knew that the third man's death warrant had just been signed.

It would be executed some day by means of a speeding truck or a bomb wired to his car's ignition, or a shotgun blast through a window or fists and feet and newspaper-wrapped lead pipe in a deserted place where nobody would hear his screams except his murderers.

It would happen just as soon as they were ready for it to happen, not a minute sooner or later. He would have to use the time that remained to him as efficiently as possible and try not to worry too much.

III

"Phonies," said the cynical bellboy.

"Honeymooners," the romantic chambermaid said firmly.

They were discussing the couple who had checked in last night at the Desert Rest Motel, Nevada.

"'Mr. and Mrs. John Smith,'" the bellboy sneered.

"Look in a phone book, wise guy. Look in any phone book, I dare you. You think there ain't any John Smiths in the whole world?"

"A shack job," said the bellboy. "And she's taking him for plenty. I seen them quiet ones before."

"I," said the chambermaid, "seen the way they look at each other..." She smiled mistily and blinked.

But as a matter of fact they were both right.

IV

The torn corpse in the snow; the doomed, calm betrayer; the happy adulterers who could make a motel chambermaid smile—we must go back one week to begin their story.

WEATHER I

It's Longitude 155 degrees, Latitude 83 degrees north. It's the Arctic Ocean, a vast plain of grinding, shifting sheets of ice under a twilight gloom. It's almost the exact middle of the six-month polar night.

There is no sound under the lead-colored sky except the booming and grinding of the ice floes. The usual howling winds of this godforsaken place have dropped to a dead calm. This is noticed by a strange little machine half-buried in a floe.

The machine is a product of the cold—here very cold—war. Of the Edison Effect, noticed and described long ago by Thomas A., who was working at the time on the problem of a practical electric light. Of a Navy-minded senator who wangled a cut in the Air Force budget, forcing generals to decide: "Since we won't have the planes or crews for patrols we'll have to do it some other way, maybe by machine." Of a huge building in New Jersey where a thousand-odd happily quarrelsome men, most of them possible geniuses and a few about whom there is no doubt whatsoever, daily turn out fundamental research and practical solutions to whatever happens to be bothering communications companies. Of a young man with a Ph.D. in mathematics who got the bright idea that finally cracked the power-lead problem; it got him a raise from $115 to $125 a week, a Class C gate pass instead of a D, and a very important note of commendation from Dr. Kelly. He valued most highly the new gate pass; it meant that he could now drop in at odd hours to tinker at his projects if he got any more bright ideas late at night or over the weekend.

The machine looks like a foot-locker and on its side, under a crust of ice, the words are stenciled: "BAROMETRIC TELEMETERING DEVICE, U.S.A.F. M-51. PROPERTY OF U. S. GOVERNMENT. DO NOT TAMPER OR DISTURB." The warning is generous. The machine is booby-trapped with an explosive charge calculated to blow up the machine and any wandering airmen or explorers who might try to pry it open and see what makes it tick.

It cost 32,000 dollars to build the machine and another 20,000-odd dollars in gasoline, salaries and overhead to parachute it to this spot from a B-50. There are hundreds like it dotted over the huge desolate plains of ice which are more or less American property.

All this money was spent so the machine could do what it's doing now. It's noticing the dead calm that has fallen on this latitude and longitude and is beeping this information southward on a tight radio beam to three airmen in a smelly little weather station on Point Anxiety, which rises from the northern coastline of Alaska.

CHAPTER III

PASSENGER JOAN LUNDBERG

"Madame Chairlady!" said Joan Lundberg.

Mrs. Quist winced and mumbled shyly: "Chair recognizes Miss Lundberg." The ladies of the Scandia Women's Democratic Club settled down or twisted uncomfortably, according as they thought Joan Lundberg was a capable and zealous party worker or a humorless fanatic.

Joan rose and said deliberately: "It seems to me that there's been a certain amount of mismanagement and last-minute maneuvering here. It's a simple question of electing one delegate to the National Conference of Democratic Women's Clubs in San Francisco. Three names have been put in nomination and we're deadlocked. Well and good; that's the American way of doing things.

"What I don't like, and I'm sure the majority of clear-thinking ladies present are with me on this point, is the way grave issues are being slurred over. We've got to send somebody to San Francisco who will make the voice of the midwest Democratic woman voter heard on such vital issues as me-tooism, squandermania, realistic curbs on the power of the labor bosses—oh, I could go on for hours!

"And what are we debating instead of these vital issues? We are debating over who will put up the better appearance. Over who will impress the ladies in San Francisco not by her determination to put a Democrat in the White House but by her clothes. Through this debate is running an ugly undertone of mink-coatism!"

They gasped at the words. The reporter from the Chicago Sun-Times drowsing in the back abruptly jerked to life and began scribbling.

"In all humbleness," said Miss Lundberg, "I ask that some friend who puts devotion to principle above appearance place my name in nomination as delegate to the National Conference of Democratic Women's Clubs. And I want to add that I'll back up my stand by paying full expenses for the trip myself and will not expect to be reimbursed by one penny for my service to the party."

There was a relieved sigh.

Mrs. Quist, too shy to run a meeting properly but serving traditionally because Mr. Quist was First Deputy Chief of the Cook County Sheriff's Police, asked timidly: "Do I hear such a nomination?"

Grinning, Edith Larsen rose and proposed Miss Lundberg as delegate. Mary Holm glared at her. Mary Holm was one of the three deadlocked candidates and knew perfectly well why Edith Larsen was spoiling her party. Edith thought Mary was making a play for her fat slob of a husband just because she'd been decently polite to him. Well, her duty was clear. Mary Holm got up, withdrew her candidacy and warmly seconded the candidacy of Joan Lundberg (the blonde frump).

Joan was elected by a comfortable margin over the required two-thirds. Most of the ladies were relieved that the treasury had been spared the burden. Joan herself was mightily relieved. Not only would she be able to show the ladies in San Francisco what a real fighting midwest Democratic clubwoman was like, but she wouldn't have to undergo the embarrassment of returning her ticket and canceling her reservation aboard the Golden Gate. Leaving nothing to chance, she had picked up the reservation that morning at Union Station. Wait too long and there might be no room left, she had sternly told herself. Take a chance—that was how our republic grew great.

The meeting adjourned for coffee and coffee-cake, and Joan was surrounded by a buzz of congratulations. Blonde, petite Mrs. Holm said gently: "I was so glad I could withdraw in favor of some really responsible person, Joan dear. You know what a burden the trip would have been for me—baby sitters, the place in a mess when I got back—Joe's a darling, but he's a bear in a den about picking up and dusting …"

(Translation: "You may have stolen my 'Frisco joy-ride from me, you blonde frump, but I've got a husband and children and you haven't.")

"I've got to pack," Joan said abruptly. "Excuse me, girls." She found her good cloth coat among the minks and leopards, and an unseen sneer curled her lip.

The reporter—he was unbelievably young—caught her at the door. "Congratulations," he said cheerily. "I'd just like to check the spelling."

She spelled her name and he put it down in block letters on a long Western Union press message form. "Do you think they'll put it on the wire?" she asked.

"Well, probably not, Miss Lundberg. We just grab a handful of these when we go out on assignment…age?"

"Thirty-two," she said.

"That was swell about mink-coatism," he said. "I'm going to put it in my lead."

"Don't bother," she said. "They'll take it out. Advertisers."

"Oh," said the young man. "I never thought of that. Are you on a paper, Miss Lundberg?"

"Excuse me," she said. "I have to pack. My train leaves at 9:05 tomorrow morning. Good-bye."

She walked from the church basement into the icy wind from the Lake, and breathed deeply. She tied on a bright, flapping babushka that softened the grim lines of her hair-do, and the wind brightened her face. Joan strode off confidently down the street. The neighborhood, unfortunately, was Republican—the staid, Scandinavian northwest side—but a woman could walk at night without being accosted. She thought of the Loop (Democratic and dangerous for women), the dreary Polish and Bohemian acres of the west side (Republican machine and dangerous) and the polyglot, pinko south side, with a shudder.

Five minutes bucking the wind brought her, flushed and panting, to the square, stark-white, red-roofed Nilsen home, no different from the other square, stark-white, red-roofed homes on both sides of the gentle-curving suburban street. She went down the little flight of concrete steps, fumbled out her key and stepped into the smothering warmth of the basement flat. They'd been closing windows again, slipping in while she was gone.

She snapped on the light and strode from one casement window to another, swinging each open a precise two inches.

Her apartment occupied half the basement. The other half contained the furnace, coal bin, a ping-pong table and usually a Nilsen or two, breathing heavily and rattling the pages of the Chicago Tribune loudly enough to be heard through the beaverboard and oak veneer of the partition.

A mumbling dialogue went on as she took off her coat, babushka, scarf and gloves.

"So she's home now, so what should I do?"

"So go tell her, lazy lump."

"So whose idea it was somebody should tell her?"

"It isn't enough I wash and cook and scrub and make over clothes for myself I have to collect the rent?"

Stertorous breathing and the rattling of the Chicago Tribune answered that. After a pause there was a firm rapping on the door between the apartment and the Nilsen commons-room.

Joan Lundberg unlocked it—the lock was a farce; Nilsen had keys both to this door and the front door, and used them whenever her back was turned—and jerked the door open viciously. "Yes, Mrs. Nilsen?" she asked.

"Please," said Mrs. Nilsen. "The rent?"

"We've been over this once, Mrs. Nilsen," Joan said. "I don't see how I could have put it plainer. I'm going to be two weeks behind in the rent because I have a fixed income and a sudden expense came up which I can't avoid. In two weeks I'll catch up and until then there's no use talking about it. Do you want me to get out?"

"I thought maybe something would come up," Mrs. Nilsen said vaguely. "What for's the expense? Maybe I can find it cheaper if it's buying."

There was a snort and a rattle of newsprint offstage.

"Nothing like that, thanks," Joan said. "I'm going on a little trip tomorrow morning and I'll be back in five days. That's all there is to it." She felt oddly reluctant to invoke politics in connection with the rent.

"Ah," said Mrs. Nilsen, looking at her middle, and retreated.

Joan closed the door and leaned tiredly against it. "She's having an abortion!" she heard Mrs. Nilsen hiss to Mr. Nilsen, who grunted and shifted in his chair, creaking.

Joan began to chuckle, and the chuckling got out of control. It grew to whoops of laughter that racked her like sobs. There was an alarmed thundering on the stairs behind the partition. The Nilsens were in full retreat from trouble. They didn't want to get involved; it was their religion. All they wanted was seventeen-fifty a week for the nicely-furnished room with bath and kitchenette, eavesdropping privileges while she was home and rights of visitation while she was gone. But they didn't want to get involved as they had often said when she was drumming up a meeting or circulating a petition.

She threw herself on the prim daybed, whooping at how wrong they were and how very, very funny it was. When the spasm passed she lay there, relaxed and sniffing occasionally, feeling light and disembodied. It had been so very, very funny, the idea of her having or needing an abortion. It was an off-color joke, but it was a joke.

Slowly she rose and went into the bathroom to undress. Dress, knitted slip moulding her, 32 bra, B cup—she squared her shoulders and squinted in the too-high medicine chest mirror. They were quite all right, she assured herself grimly even if she didn't wear indecent uplift bras like the kept wives at the Club. If what you wanted was to do your bit to save the nation from its enemies foreign and domestic, a sound grasp of parliamentary law was more to the point.

She unhooked the garter belt, incongruous satin over faded, tired, thigh-length snuggies going into their third Chicago winter, and peeled off her stockings. The snuggies were bulky. Of course that was where Mrs. Nilsen had got her brilliant idea. You try to keep sensibly warm in a Chicago winter and dirty-minded old so-and-so's conclude that you're a loose woman. As if she had the time for such nonsense!

Under the snuggies her belly was flat. Perhaps not good enough to win any prizes, but certainly not bad enough to get her kicked out of bed by a reasonable man—

Startled at the trend of her thoughts, she snatched her dressing gown from the hook on the door and belted it firmly around her. That was that. Cover the body and forget about it.

Virtuously she washed her underwear in the bathroom sink and draped it to dry along the shower-curtain rod, dropped a little-girl printed flannel nightgown over her head and went to bed.

She couldn't sleep.

The old fool's hissed accusation still rang in her ears. Twisting on the narrow bed she thought: if I went in for that kind of thing I wouldn't have an abortion. If I got caught I'd go someplace in the southwest where they don't make a fuss about legitimacy on the birth certificates and I'd have the baby and bring him up. We could live on the income and maybe get one of those adobe houses in Taos cheaper than this place and I could brush up on my piano and try painting again. Of course party work would be out, so the whole thing's out of the question. First things first; there aren't enough of us to squander our time.

She thought of her father for the first time in weeks and clearly saw in the dark the thin, cynical face which had been so attractive to so many women; she heard in the silence the thin, cynical voice that charmed them with its cruel wit and grace. What fools they were! she thought violently. If they'd lived with him as long as I had to they would have known better. But they never did. They came and went, and she was always there and he was always graceful and brilliant and mocking until she wanted to scream: Be dull for an hour, can't you? Be kind and normal for just a little while or I'll go crazy! I can't keep up with it!

Well, she brooded, her wish had come true. Throat cancer, inoperable, had made him quite dull for eighteen months, and then he was gone, following the mysterious figure of her mother into limbo.

Thank God there had been hard work and Americanism to fight for after that. Thank God she had inherited some of his diabolical word-brilliance and none of his twisted ethics. Thank God there was work for her to do in the world.

She fell comfortably asleep at last.

Upstairs the Nilsens buzzed and muttered, wondering who the man was.

WEATHER II

It's Point Anxiety, Alaska, a miserable ice-covered promontory of the northern coast. Three airmen in a corrugated-iron shack which sprouts tall radio masts are the total population. They are young, because young men resist the cold best; older men tend to get frozen gums if they step outside.

All three are volunteers. One wants the extra money for the hardship duty; he's going to open a cleaning shop in Cincinnati when he gets out; he already has $3,752 in his postal savings account. Another's motive is religious; he is fighting the antichrist by serving devotedly and well in the most difficult and disagreeable post he can find. The third is a kind-hearted young man who happens to be a "situational murderer." A field hand scared his sister, he went to have a talk with the buck and before he knew it the field hand was dying of a fractured skull. His pastor and the sheriff were understanding; no purpose would be served by spoiling his young life over an accident that could have happened to anybody. But they thought he'd better get out of the county for a while in case snoopers turned up with questions. He got out; way out.

The three young men play poker endlessly; it is hard for them to communicate in any other way. The cleaner-and-dyer-to-be could tell them about spotting with $KMnO_4$, about steaming velveteens, about his revolutionary idea for three-color plastic advertising garment hangers, but they would only smile blankly and ask if he wanted some coffee. The religious young man could hardly share with them his dawning discovery there in the Arctic waste that he had a vocation; they would not even recognize the word. And the third young man's horizon was entirely bounded by the raising of soybeans, the training of hound dogs, the protection of womanhood.

They went through basic training at Sampson Air Force Base on Lake Cayuga in New York; being intelligent, they were forwarded to the Weather Technician School at Wright-Patterson Air Force Base, Dayton, Ohio. There, in six grinding months, they learned to operate the complex radio and meteorological equipment which surrounds them here as they play poker.

An urgent beep-beep-beep from one of the radio receivers breaks into a three-dollar pot. They put down their hands automatically and get to work. They release balloons and follow them across the lead-colored sky with telescopes that give bearing and elevation at one-second intervals. They set the figures on a special circular slide-rule as big as a table-top, adding in temperature, wind velocity and barometric pressure. They shoot the result by radio to the big base at White Horse, Yukon Territory. It takes them about an hour, and then they pick up their poker hands again.

One of them draws to four hearts and fills his flush. His fatal poker habit is talking to hide his excitement over a good hand. "That's a son of a bitch coming up," he says.

The others, who know his fatal habit, feel relieved and drop their hands. They pick up the conversation and agree that it is indeed a bad son of a bitching norther rolling down from the Arctic Ocean.

They shuffle and deal again while the leaden sky outside flowers down and a small shrill wind blows hard from the ocean, bringing with it the first snowflakes of the norther.

CHAPTER IV

PASSENGER FOREMAN

Thin January sunlight slanted through the dirty windows of the Chicago Bureau of the World Wireless Press Service. Bureau Chief Hal Foreman looked on his newsroom and found it good. George and Johnny, teletype operators, were pounding out respectively, the general and sports copy. Goldberg and—what's his name?—Adams were respectively ripping news from the latest editions of the Chicago papers and rewriting it to move on the WW wire. The receiving printer from New York was clicking out Washington and foreign news, and the Las Vegas Western Union telemeter was, thank God, closed down this week for some reason or other.

Everything was beautifully under control and he went for his coat to get some coffee. Shrugging into the coat, he heard a brisk, impersonal clang-clang from the New York printer.

Johnny called out sharply, not looking up from his racing copy or letting his flying fingers slow on the keys: "Note from New York, Hal!"

He went to the printer and read: "CH CHF-WARAMA-RANGU MIDAS WAGOGO SLUMMY IMMY-JC."

All he understood of it was that it was a note for him—"CH CHF"—from WW's president, Jefferson Clark, who wanted something done "IMMY"—immediately—about a phone number—"MIDAS." The rest was front-office code, distinct from newsroom code. He ripped the note off the machine and brought it into the business office adjoining the small newsroom.

Miss Sillery looked up icily from a yellow-paged ledger.

"I'm sorry to trouble you, Madge," Foreman said, "but could you break this for me?"

She nodded bitterly and Foreman retreated to the newsroom in his overcoat to wait. The printer from National Press popped erratically and much too slowly. He frowned as he saw slowly emerging: "6TH NEW ORLEANS OFF 03—MONEYMAN, LA SPECTRE & FOTO" and then immediately: "6TH NEW ORLEANS BILSAB IS 3RD." Foreman glanced at the big wall clock, which showed twenty-one minutes past the hour. Eighteen minutes to get the flash up from the Fair Grounds. Stinking time. And the way the foto result had followed right on the heels of the flash looked even lousier. Somebody had held the flash up somewhere along the line, no damn doubt of that.

Johnny's fingers rippled smoothly over the keys of his teletype as, with his head craned at an impossible angle, he copied the flash and foto from the National Press printer.

"Johnny," Foreman asked, "how's Fair Grounds today?"

"Stinks," the operator replied briefly. "Fifteen minutes, twenty minutes, eighteen minutes. The third was past-post."

"Um," Foreman said, and moved away. He'd have to see National Press, which he didn't like to do. National Press had been much in the newspapers lately. It seems that along with supplying racing news to legitimate sources, they did business with bookies and some Senators did not approve. So far the tar-brush had missed WW.

He stalled for a while by reading the New York report. The machine was printing what looked very much like a long, dull, unedited story right from their Reuters ticker about the long-term effects of pound-devaluation on gold-mining in the Rand, South Africa. Fascinating, Foreman thought sourly. Just what the clients are panting to hear. This goddam outfit is becoming a laughingstock. At the last luncheon meeting of the Chicago Radio Newsmen's Association he had been on the defensive for an hour. The boys had bored in good-humoredly, wanting to know who was buying the report these days and why. It had been difficult to answer. The New York office didn't tell him things. The only client they had in Chicago was WJC, and that was only because old Wally Irvine, their news director, had a sentimental and somewhat superstitious attachment to WW. He'd stuck with them for fifteen years, he could stick with them for fifteen more. There was always AP-Radio, UP and the INS wire for him to fall back on if WW let him down on a newscast. But old Wally had missed the meeting, home sick, and the going had been rough.

The hell with it. He had a job to do.

He took out his notebook, looked up National's number and dialed it at a rewrite phone in the corner. "Illinois Turf Digest," said a woman's cheery voice.

"Mr. Charny, please."

Long pause. "Who is this calling?"

"Foreman. World Wireless."

"One mo-ment." It was a long moment. Those guys claimed they were a legitimate business and they couldn't help it if crooks bought their service any more than a newspaper could help it if a bookie read results in their turf edition. But they were hard as hell to get hold of. Somebody picked up a phone at the other end and Foreman heard the machine-gun rattle of a dozen Morse sounders going full blast in the distance.

"Yuh?" said somebody. It wasn't Charny's voice.

"Let me talk to Charny."

Long pause. "Who's this?"

"Foreman. World Wireless."

"I'll try to gettum. Hold the line."

The next voice was Charny's. "Hi, Bill!" he said brightly. "What can I do for you?"

"If you really want to know, you can snap things up from New Orleans. You past-posted us on the third race. And I just watched the sixth come in. It was awful. The flash with a photo for third, and then the photo result right after it. Not a second between them. You can't tell me he wasn't copying them all off the same card. And his punching, just incidentally, was lousy. When I see punching like that it scares the juice out of me because anybody that bad is going to make mistakes in the figures."

Charny roared with laughter. "Don't take it so hard, Bill!" he said. "I'll tell you what it is. He's kind of a new man, he's been doing other work, so we're just breaking him in on the printers."

Foreman said, knowing he shouldn't: "Why don't you one time break a new man in on a horse-room wire instead of on us?"

Charny said, in a completely different voice: "Okay. We'll pull him off your machine. If there's anything else, call me. Good-bye."

Me and my big mouth, Foreman thought. If they pull a slow-down on us there'll be hell to pay. Well, it's too late now. He wondered what kind of other work the new man had been doing before they put him on the printers: wig-wagging results from a park to a confederate in a nearby house? Manning an abandoned Postal Telegraph "dry wire" with battery and key? Building switchboards that would hook together thirty phones acquired through dummies into what the newspapers always called a "nerve center of gambling"?

He wandered over to the National printer again. The punching style had changed. Crisp, regular and authoritative, the letters clicked onto the paper at a good 50 w.p.m.: "SIXTH SUNSHINE OK BALLAMAN 4.40 3.20 2.80 GARBOYLE 19.40 (OK) 8.80 RUNAMILE 2.20 TIME 147 3/5 OFF 17½."

Things were under control again for the time being. Now if the note wasn't another headache he could go and get that coffee.

Miss Sillery handed him a page from one of her three-by-five pads on which she had written, in her precise script, with one of her needle-pointed pencils: "Chicago Bureau Chief, call me immediately at National 0323 from an outside phone. Jefferson Davis Clark."

"Thank you, Madge," he said, studying it. "Uh, that's a Washington number, isn't it?" It wasn't any of the Washington bureau numbers, though.

"Mr. Clark is in Washington this week," she said. She knew things like that. You had to go to her all the time for bits of information. A client's address. Rates and costs. Where you could get in touch with Clark. Who was new in New York and Washington. What clients were added and who had canceled.

"Thanks," he said, and headed for the newsroom petty cash box, locked in a filing cabinet that also contained the bureau's skimpy and decrepit morgue. He scooped out twelve quarters and scribbled a slip. He'd never got a message like that before. There had been a good deal of: "You alone, Hal?" and "You suah theah's nobody else on the lahn?" before proceeding to a conversation about, usually, sports wire clients and the need for speed. But never any of this outside-phone stuff.

He slid into a booth at the corner cigar store and called long distance. She ordered him to deposit one-fifty and he sent the quarters pouring into the phone in a clanging stream.

"Hello?" said a guarded voice with a southern drawl that he recognized.

"Hello, Mr. Clark. This is Foreman in Chicago. What can I do for you?"

"You calling from an outside phone like I tole you?"

"Yes, sir. Corner cigar store."

"Okeh. You got a pencil and paper?"

"Sure." He worked them out of his inside breast pocket. "Shoot."

"Take this down. Room 1423, Monongahela Buildin'. You know wheah that is?"

"Sure."

"Take this down. Mr. Ganyon. G-A-N-Y-O-N. Eight o'clock tonight. Got that? You go an' see Mr. Ganyon at Room 1423 Monongahela Buildin' at eight o'clock tonight."

From an easy-going, frankly sloppy guy like Clark it was astounding. Foreman repeated the details of the appointment.

"Good. Now, Hal, Mr. Ganyon's people are very good, very valuable friends of ouah's. I took the liberty of tellin' them that you'd be glad to do a job for them. It may take you out of town for sever'l days, but that cain't be helped."

"But the Bureau!" said Foreman, startled. "All I have is Goldberg and three green men!"

"To hell with the Bureau!" Clark said dispassionately. "Put Goldberg in charge an' don't worry about it. Take on another buck-an-hour kid. Is Backmeister still theah?"

That was Johnny. "Yes, sure."

"He's a good man. Don't worry about a thing. Hal, I recommended you up to the hilt to these very, very good friends of ouah's. I said you were intelligent, I said you could take orders an' I said you could keep youah mouth shut. I went right down the lahn for you and I trust you won' let me down."

"Well, Mr. Clark, what's all this about?"

"All I'm free to say at this tahm is that it's related to ouah Las Vegas operation. Well, that's all for now. You'll heah the rest from the party I mentioned. Good-bye, Hal. See you some time."

Click.

Foreman went back upstairs to the bureau without getting his cup of coffee. Goldberg was pounding out a story. Foreman waited until he was finished and said: "Sam, I may be going away for a few days. You'll be in charge of the Bureau. I don't think there's anything coming up in the way of installations, sales or supplies. If anything you can't handle turns up, just spike it for me."

Goldberg's dark face was shining with incredulous joy, "Sure, Hal!" he said earnestly. "Why, this is marvelous! The experience will be wonderful!"

Foreman smiled back meagerly and shucked his overcoat. You got to do everything at WW. The pay wasn't much, but the experience was wonderful. He studied the idle Las Vegas teleprinter broodingly. For two months it had been a rush-rush priority to get the race results on it first and fully. Nominally there was another World Wireless bureau at the other end. Nominally. This was when there had been shootings and a crackdown in California.

Goddamn it, Foreman yelled silently, how the hell did I get mixed up in this anyhow?

But he knew how. He had got mixed up in it by pretending you could get something for nothing, that the experience would be marvelous, that it was just a lot of talk in the newspapers, that WW was a brave little firm battling the giant news monopolies, that Charny was a jolly good fellow, that he was just a little guy following orders.

So quit the job, he said. Go in and tell Madge Sillery you're through and for her to mail you your check and withholding statement. No; you can't do that. You bought a suit that isn't paid for yet and you have a lease on the apartment and you're having a good time with the girls and you like seafood cocktails and steaks. No; you can't do that. You'd be a bum on the street with maybe five hundred other unemployed newsmen tramping from City News Bureau to the Sun-Times to the Trib to the AP to the News to the UP to the Herald-American to the neighborhood papers and never finding anything. No; you can't quit. Just hang on, Hal Foreman told himself. Everything will probably turn out all right.

He looked up a number and called it. A young-sounding voice answered.

"This is Mr. Foreman at World Wireless. Minelli, are you still looking for newswork?"

"Sure am, Mr. Foreman. Did something—?"

"Yeah. Come on down."

He read the Trib for three-quarters of an hour. When Minelli arrived, a skinny, intense fellow of 22 or so, he received him in the shoe-box private office he hardly ever used.

"We have a couple of weeks of desk work at a dollar an hour. It isn't much, but I'm sure you know what the experience means."

"Of course, Mr. Foreman. What would the work involve?"

"You'd be rewrite man under Mr. Goldberg—I'm going to be out of town. Essentially you take dispatches from various sources, put them into WW style and get them on the wire."

The boy's face fell. "No reporting at all?"

"Very little reporting out of here. We rely mostly on our string men and the local papers."

"Local papers. How's that, Mr. Foreman?"

Foreman couldn't meet his eye as he said: "We clip them and rewrite."

"Clip—I don't understand you. You mean we take their news—"

"Sure that's what I mean," Foreman said. "You got any objections?"

Minelli looked dubious. "I thought you couldn't do that, Mr. Foreman."

He looked kindly. "Theoretically, no. But everybody does, and don't let them kid you otherwise. You don't go around bragging about it, but you do it anyway. I could tell you stories that would curl your hair, Minelli."

The boy laughed dutifully. "If you say it's okay, Mr. Foreman. I guess they don't teach you everything in journalism school."

The rest of the interview was pep-talk. He sent Minelli away happy.

Foreman walked out of the office to have dinner before his appointment and Goldberg, still beaming, wished him a cheery good-night.

* * * *

Office buildings are like cities. Your jerkwater town or your fifth-rate little building is shut tight by eight o'clock. It takes heroic measures to get action. But in a metropolis or a great office building there's no closing hour. Somebody's always up, lights are always on. An elevator man took Foreman to the fourteenth floor of the Monongahela Building without surprise.

Room 1423 had chastely lettered in gold leaf on its frosted-glass door: Dearborn Real Estate Co. Far down in the lower left-hand corner of the frosted-glass plate was lettered in small, plain black: N.P.-Chi. National Press, of course, and small enough to be mistakable for the initials of the sign-painting company.

He went in. It was the conventional receptionist's window and the conventional three-by-six waiting room with an electrolier, etchings on the wall and green leather chairs. The magazines on the end table were solid real-estate stuff: The Journal of Appraisals; N.A.R.B. Digest of State Legislation. Foreman pressed a button and sat down a little gratefully, in one of the green leather chairs. He had drunk three martinis before having a seafood cocktail and a steak.

It was not a conventional receptionist who appeared behind the window. "Grocer," Foreman thought instantly when he saw it. It was a long Italian face needing a shave. It looked incomplete without a white apron. You could easily see it smiling over peaches or green peppers. The illusion evaporated when it said in a voice cold as steel and unaccented: "Who do you want to see?"

Foreman got up. "Mr. Ganyon," he said. "I'm Hal Foreman from World Wireless."

The face continued to stare.

"Mr. Clark arranged an appointment for me," Foreman added.

It vanished without a word. After thirty seconds the newsman picked up a copy of The Journal of Appraisals and pretended to read it. After two minutes the door opened and the man with a grocer's face said: "Follow me."

Foreman followed him through an outer office made hazardous by eight oak desks, treading softly on grey broadloom. (The sale had been made three years ago by a Mr. Boyce.) He followed him into a secretary's office and then into a large oak-paneled office where there were three men.

Into the silence he said: "I have an appointment with Mr. Ganyon."

One of the men, beefy and red-faced, said with a secret smile: "Ganyon couldn't make it. I'll talk to him. Did Mr. Clark explain that this was a very, very important matter and a very confidential one?"

"Yes," Foreman said, frightened. There was the beefy, red-faced man and there were two other men who looked like brothers. They were blond, clean-cut—and somehow indescribably nasty.

"Sit down," the red-faced man said. "Let's talk turkey. I'm not a smart man with the words. I'm just an old circulation slugger who's been lucky. And I want to stay lucky. But I know enough not to stick my neck out.

"Mr. Foreman, I understand you know the wire-service game?" He said it with a secret smile.

"Something about it," Foreman admitted, frightened.

"What's the difference between a duplex and a simplex A.T.&T. lease f'rinstance?"

Foreman told him, and the red-faced man smiled with pleasure. It was the beginning of an hour-long inquisition covering A.T.&T. leases, the

Western Union hierarchy, the old Postal Telegraph dry wires, nomenclature of the Bell System engineering force, maintenance service, telemetering line charges and hours, the going rate for teletype operators and steady Morse men, how to spot a no-questions-asked office building and many more things which Foreman was startled to discover that he knew.

"Excellent," the red-faced man pronounced at last. "What we want for you to do is contact a certain party in San Francisco. This party wants a news bureau set up for him, mostly on the sports side, with maybe twelve drops in and around town. This party is just going into the news bureau business and he doesn't know the ins and outs. All he knows is he wants to go into the news bureau business and he has sense enough to pay high for a high-class source of news. We want for you to handle the technical details. If it's politics, he can help you but the plain spade-work is all yours. We want for you to set up an economical system for him—but you know all that. Watch your hours, watch your hiring, watch your rentals and you'll be okay. You'll get the dope from this party on addresses and things like that. All I have to tell you is that the line to the main bureau in Frisco will run from WW Chicago six A.M. to midnight. There won't be any trouble, will there?"

Foreman could see it very plainly. National Press, very much in the clear. World Wireless hopelessly compromised in case of a breakdown. The only link between National and the Frisco distributor of racing news this meeting here and now—

"I don't like it," he said.

Pause.

"Maybe Clark didn't tell you all you needed to know," the red-faced man said gently. "Maybe he didn't tell you that he gets three thousand a week for six years, which is close to a million bucks. Didn't you handle the Las Vegas standby telemeter, kid?"

"Yes," said Foreman.

"So what's the bitch? They drilled Cohen, the heat went on, you set up a Las Vegas telemeter. Don't tell me you can't add two and two, kid." The voice was infinitely persuasive.

"I can add two and two," Foreman said. "I still don't like it. I'm getting out of here." He started for the door, but the man with the grocer's face was standing there.

The beefy man said: "Like hell you are, kid. You got the wrong idea."

The man with a grocer's face caught Foreman a terrific blow in the belly, without seeming to try hard. The newsman collapsed on the broadloom carpet, doubled up and crowing harshly. The two men who looked like brothers moved in. One of them picked Foreman up and held him under the armpits. The other slugged his right fist into the newsman's midriff again and again, expressionless. Foreman rocked and grunted under the blows, powerless to do anything except feel the exploding fire of each deliberate piledriver slam.

The room was a red haze before him when he heard a voice: "That's enough, kids. That's enough, you queer sons of bitches! Leave him alone, I want to talk to him."

He was dumped on a leather couch and a glass of ice-water splashed into his face. It jerked him upright, staring.

"Take it easy, kid," the red-faced man told him. "I want you to see some pictures." He snapped his fingers and one of the men who looked like brothers snickered and pulled from his inside breast pocket a parcel of snapshots. Foreman was quite sure they would be obscene pictures, wild though the thought was, from his manner.

They were obscene only in a certain sense. The first showed a drowned man with many stab-wounds in him. There were crabs eating his face away. The man with the photographs, in a somewhat high-pitched voice, delivered a running commentary.

"This one was with the ice-pick. Ice-pick isn't good because wounds like that swell shut with the congestion and decomposition gas forms in the body cavities and it floats up… This one was with the razor, which was better but still not the answer… This one was the cleaver. You see what a bad Wop did to him. A bad Wop is the worst thing to have working on you there is… Blowtorch… This is another blowtorch but the people had more time. Three hours, somebody told me… Battery acid, this one—"

Foreman looked and listened in a dull comprehension that he would do exactly what these people wanted.

After looking at all the photographs he told them that.

"Good," said the red-faced man. "I hated to see you act like a God-damned fool, Foreman. Here's the expense money." It was five hundred dollars in small, worn bills. "It should hold you for a month. Here's your ticket and reservation." It was a roomette on the Golden Gate. The penciled scribble on the envelope said it left tomorrow morning at 9:05. "And when you're located in Frisco, you just phone Mr. Clark and he'll give you the name of the party we want you to contact. And, uh, you needn't think any of this is going to get out, kid. We'll tell 'em you were reasonable right from the start."

Foreman was wearily sure that the red-faced man was embarrassed, not for himself, but because he, Foreman, had made a fool of himself.

"That's all right," he said, and got up, aching. The man with a grocer's face walked with him silently to the elevator. In his uncomfortable company Foreman jeered at himself bitterly: So you wanted something for nothing?

He walked the dark streets for two hours that night, aching and filled with self-loathing. I'll get out of it, he told himself over and over again. I won't have anything to do with pimps and killers and dope-runners. I'll get out of it. They bribe and steal and murder but they can't make me over. I'll get out of it.

At 1:30, aching and filled with self-loathing, he went home and packed.

CHAPTER V

SNOW

This is White Horse, Yukon Territory, Dominion of Canada. It is 750 miles south of the smelly little weather station on Point Anxiety, but in January it is still a frozen desolation. Here winterized B-50's land and take off endlessly, winterized jeeps and weasels crawl endlessly through the snow-plowed streets loaded with winterized Canadian and U. S. airmen.

A weatherman, perspiring in a shack overheated by its oil-drum stove, pushes back his R.C.A.F. cap and says: "Here comes a bloody blow, say the Yanks at Anxiety. Get the leftenant, will you?"

The lieutenant, a Ph.D. who never thought that specializing in the physics of the air would lead to the King's commission and duty in this godforsaken hole, studies the dispatch from Point Anxiety, studies several other dispatches and sketches a sinuous line in red on the big hemisphere map.

"Flash it on, Jock," he says. "I've got to go and tell the Air Commander."

Jock grins sympathetically and makes a curious cranking gesture like a machinist reaming out a drilled hole. The lieutenant nods wryly, squares his shoulders and leaves.

"Goddamn it, man!" the Air Commander says a few minutes later, "you weather people can't ground my planes for three days!"

"I know I can't sir," the lieutenant told him, "but that norther sure as hell can."

"But I've got twelve boys to qualify as multi-engine winterized pilots before February, familiarization courses for forty-three Yank interceptor pilots, the Parliamentary commission on my neck and the regular patrolling... how much time have we?"

"We'll be zero-zero in six hours, sir. And snowbound in twelve."

The Air Commander mutters incoherently and waves the lieutenant from his office. The lieutenant grins in the corridor and goes to the radar room. There on the twelve-inch screen he can already see crawling down from the north a glowing, pale-green film which is the radar signal for snow—immense quantities of snow.

CHAPTER VI

PASSENGER MONA GREER

Mona Greer was leaving in the morning for San Francisco where "Bozzy" Hartman would hold an autographing party for her in his Candle-light Bookshop. It would be a nice shot in the arm for her Thighs of the Wild Mare, which was sagging salewise now that the fuss about its alleged indecency was subsiding. Not that she needed the money.

Naturally there was a going-away party, and naturally Maggie Buckle threw it in her Gold Coast duplex.

Early in the evening, before half the guests had arrived, a naïve visiting book critic from New York muttered to his wife: "For Christ's sake, let's get out of here. They're all fruits. I don't take this crap in New York and I'm not going to take it in Chicago."

His wife said: "Oh, I don't know, Harry. Mona's kind of sweet."

"She was stroking your hand and looking at you with rape in her eye, if that's what you mean. Get your coat and I'll go tell that Buckle woman you have a headache."

Their departure was unnoticed. There were so many really simpatica people there that one depressingly dull couple from the East wasn't missed. Mona embalmed them in a honeyed epigram that highlighted their literary and sexual provincialism, and made Maggie Buckle shriek with laughter.

Erect as a queen, slim and unlined, looking by candlelight only half her forty years, Mona moved smilingly through the throng of guests and sat beside a dark, pretty little girl who was watching the scene wide-eyed and a little forlorn, twirling a champagne glass.

"Hello, little one," Mona said. "What's your name?" Her voice was queenly, too; a warm contralto with smiling notes in it.

"Rosa Bonomo," the child said. "You're Miss Greer, aren't you? I came with Jack Shoemaker. He was going to introduce me to you, but he seems to have got lost."

Mona had seen Jack Shoemaker, a blond butch from Northwestern, with his arm around a delicate fellow who taught Art at the U. of C. Evidently it was all new to the child. "Tell me," she said, "what do you do."

"Sculpture—some day, I hope," the child said. "I'm at Northwestern but it's just a damn waste of time. I want to go East, maybe to Italy. Dad's a stone-cutter. He says Italy's the place to learn sculpture—but I suppose you know all that, Miss Greer. You used to do sculpture yourself. I was going to ask you whether you've given it up."

"Call me Mona, dear," Mona said. "I gave it up because I was vain and foolish. Sculpture nowadays takes more than talent and hard work; it takes heroism. Aristede Maillol told me once—"

"You knew Maillol?" Rosa Bonomo gasped.

"Oh, dear. I'm afraid I dropped a name, didn't I? Yes, I studied under him for a year in Paris. At the end of the year he looked at my hands—no callouses. He showed me his—like shoeleather. And he threw me out of his studio, never to darken its door again. Let me see your hands, little one."

Rosa Bonomo worshipfully entrusted her hands to the woman who had studied under the great Aristede Maillol. Mona gently manipulated them, saying: "Strong. Capable. Sculptor's hands, without a doubt." She knew the child's breath was quickening and that little tremors were traveling up her arms, and she knew also when to stop. "Maillol was such a funny old fellow, in spite of his genius. He detested plaster-casters because he thought they were all robbers. There was one full-size nude he worked on and worked on and added to until naturally it was too weak to be taken to the exhibit without shattering."

"Yes, I know," Rosa Bonomo said breathlessly. "I read about that in Davidson's book. Have you read it, Miss Greer—Mona?"

"Davidson? No. I was never very interested in Jo. He was witty, but those busts of his—photography, little one. Not sculpture." Her queenly smile of affection took the sting out of the judgment. But as a matter of fact she had read Jo Davidson's book and had got the anecdote about Maillol out of it. It was as close as she had ever come to Maillol, but the child couldn't be expected to understand that. What a pretty little thing she was, with firm little breasts—

"Little one," she said, "are you really interested in my sculpture?"

"Of course, Mona!"

"Then let's run away. I have a few pieces still in my place, five minutes from here. They haven't been admired for ages. Let's slip out and slip back; I'd love to have you see them."

The child was overwhelmingly flattered and flustered. "Good heavens, Mona. What a thing to do. Your own party! And what would Jack think if he looked around for me?" But she giggled.

"Let's go, little one," Mona smiled, and they went. There were speculative looks cast at the woman and the girl threading their way, smiling, to the cloakroom, but no looks of surprise.

The doorman whistled up a taxi for them while they stood inside. They were exposed to the icy wind off the Lake for only a few seconds.

They sat close in the taxi, talking little.

Mona was not such a fool as to think the child was entering the she-wolf's scented den as a wide-eyed innocent. Not nowadays. Nowadays the young men were wary of the benevolent interest of an older man. The pretty little girls nowadays kept their guard up against a woman's friendship that was in any way ambiguous. Little Miss Muffet, beside her in the taxi, knew quite well that there was a distinct possibility and was running a calculated risk. One's fame and one's charm were weighed against the chance that Little Miss Muffet might find herself pursued around a table by a female Harpo Marx, or having to say cutting things in order to get away intact. Of one thing Little Miss Muffet was sure: there might be an undignified scene, but of course there was no possibility at all that she would succumb. They were all very sure of that, Mona mused, smiling.

Mona let them in with a key. "No maid," she said, smiling. "The complications an artist undergoes with servants are endless. Either they are sternly disapproving or they become emotionally involved."

That, little one, is to let you know that I know. It's not strong enough to send you screaming from the house, nor is it so weak that you can honestly say later that you didn't know.

"I see," Rosa Bonomo said after a pause. "What a nice place you have!"

"Thank you. Drop your coat and have a drink. This is Green Chartreuse, which is bad for the figure and much too strong. You'd better have a sherry."

"Please," the girl said. Mona poured the sherry for the girl and a pony of the fiery green syrup for herself.

They raised glasses solemnly, and Rosa Bonomo cried, startled: "Why, it's the exact color of your eyes! How extraordinary!"

"Little one," Mona confided, "that's the only reason why I drink the bloody stuff." They laughed and drank, and Mona said: "Come and see my relics."

They were dotted about the apartment. There were seven pieces, all table-size, all carved stone. Three were abstractions, three were female nudes in the fluid Rodin manner and one was a group of two nude women, ambiguously entwined.

Rosa Bonomo took it all very seriously, studying the pieces from all angles and cocking her head much but saying little. Finally: "Technically they're perfect, Mona. And you know what a lot that means nowadays. You didn't try to get away with anything. I like them. They're very serious, first-rate work. And your versatility is amazing. The technique of each piece might belong to a different sculptor."

Mona suppressed a start. The child knew what she was talking about. A different sculptor had done each piece—a thing one could almost forget fifteen years later and an ocean away from Paris.

"Thank you," she said. "Simply and humbly, thank you. I do value your criticism."

The girl flushed with pleasure, and then looked alarmed. Mona had dropped into a chair, her face drawn. "What's the matter?" she asked.

"An old football injury," Mona said, smiling through the mask of pain. "When I scored the winning run against the Carlyle Indians for Harvard in '03. You youngsters can't take it any more. We never heard of shoulder-guards or helmets in those days."

"Don't talk nonsense, Mona," the girl cried crossly. "Is there anything I can do?"

"Have a drink with me and help me to bed. It's migraine. I wouldn't wish it on my publisher. Not even on my agent."

Rosa Bonomo looked undecided and poured sherry and chartreuse at the cellarette. She sipped her drink nervously as Mona gulped half of hers. "Better," said Mona. "Thank you." There was another spasm of pain across her face and the suspended liqueur glass twitched and poured the rest of the chartreuse on her right breast.

"Messy stuff," Mona said, lying back against the chair with her eyes closed and a half smile on her lips.

"Let me," the girl said. She dabbed at the stain with a dinky handkerchief from her evening bag. It was not quite a caress.

"You're being very sweet, little one," Mona said. "Get me to bed, please." She put her arm around the child and felt the quicker breathing. The Little Miss Muffets were all so sure they hadn't an ounce of it in them; they were all so surprised to find themselves responding… but you must never drive them to an irrevocable act until there's no retreat.

In the bedroom Mona sat at her vanity table and Rosa Bonomo, without words, began to unbutton her dress at the back while she leisurely removed necklace, small watch and dinner ring.

"Does it last long? The migraine?" Rosa Bonomo asked, strainedly.

Mona stepped out of her dress and sleeked her black satin slip down over her belly and thighs, slowly. "Sometimes a masseuse helps me," she said. "I'll be all right. You get back to the party, little one." She drew the slip over her head and stood in bra and garter belt and stockings, shining black satin, creamy skin and the sheer caress of nylon.

She went to the bed and lay face down on the coverlet. It was better not to look at Little Miss Muffet now while she was weighing her calculated risk, troubled by the startling new thing she felt, able almost to believe that everything was quite all right, thinking that Mona Greer was the most wonderful person she had ever met—

"I could help you," the girl said in a strained, dry voice.

Very naturally, Mona told her: "That would be very sweet of you, little one. The back of my neck, kneading, not too hard…ah, that's very sweet… you have such clever hands, little one… it's nice, isn't it? Awfully nice… you've never done this before, have you? Are you shy?"

"A little," the girl said almost in a whisper. Her caressing hands slid helplessly over the creamy shoulders.

"I'll turn the light down, little one." There was the bedside cord that turned off the dressing-table lamps.

In the warm darkness Mona said, smiling secretly: "That's nicer, isn't it darling? Ah, you're very sweet …" She turned over languidly. "Don't stop, darling…ah, isn't this nice? You aren't shy any more, are you?"

"No," the girl whispered in the dark. "No, no, no!"

"Let me, darling," Mona said. Her hand climbed Rosa Bonomo's arm like a serpent and felt it stiffen in fright and disgust for a split-second, and then the child was on the bed in her arms. Undressing her was an exciting game in which she always resisted and always yielded as Mona's warm hands slid slowly over her firm young curves…

With a hoarse cry, it ended for Rosa Bonomo. She lay like one dead for minutes and then began to sob slowly and without hope.

"Why darling, what's the matter?" asked Mona brightly, grinning like a she-wolf in the dark.

The child sat up on the bed, sobbing: "My God, what am I going to do? What am I going to do?"

"Darling," yawned Mona, deliciously tired and relaxed, "you're going to wash up, put on your little things and leave. You were perfectly delightful, but now I'm so-o-o-o sleepy."

"You dirty old bitch!" Rosa Bonomo screamed.

"Am I, now? Shall I tell you exactly what you are, little one? And not in medical language either?" She told her, spitting out the blunt harsh, anglo-saxon words.

"I'll go to the police," wept the girl.

"Yes, darling. You do that. Tell them all about us. Draw them diagrams if you like, clearly labeled. But first will you clear out of here? I'm leaving for San Francisco in the morning and I'm sle-e-e-epy." She twisted luxuriously on the bed.

The child was struggling into her clothes in the dark, afraid or ashamed to ask for a light. Mona heard her stump through the apartment and slam the door.

What a lovely going-away present she had been, Mona thought drowsily. And what nice little girls might be waiting for her in San Francisco. And perhaps even on the train one might find…

CHAPTER VII

SNOW

The stationmaster's office was a cool retreat from the scurrying, crowded confusion of the great vaulted concourse. Mr. Bemis looked out over the arrivals and departures in his charge for a moment before he turned again to the teletyped dispatch on his desk.

It was a weather advisory from the Western Division, which expected snow in the Rockies—possibly a hell of a lot of snow. There was no indication as to what he was supposed to do about it. Western Division was simply covering itself for the record.

Mr. Bemis watched the telautograph pencil jog out a note: GOLDEN GATE ZPRESS DEPRTURE FIVE MINS ON SKED. DELAY AWAIT DEVELOPMNTS WEATHER PICTURE? MORRIS.

And that was Mr. Morris, the dispatcher, simply covering himself for the record.

Mr. Bemis tapped his teeth with a pencil, grabbed his phone and called up the line to Denver. His opposite number in the Union Station there said to him irritably: "How should I know, Bemis? We're completely overcast here, we have about half an inch of powdery snow so far and no sign of a let-up. All our plows are in working order and we've got the crews if we have to use them. That's all I know."

Bemis thanked him and hung up. "Hell," he said at last. "This ain't a God-damned airline." He took the telautograph pencil and scribbled: THE GOLDEN GATE EXPRESS WILL LEAVE ON SCHEDULE.

And leaned back a little breathlessly, wondering if it would arrive on schedule.

CHAPTER VIII

LUNCHEON

Boyce settled back as the train glided smoothly out of the station. His head was aching a little from last night. And his wife had not even got out of bed to make him breakfast.

Covertly he glanced at the blonde slim girl who shared his seat. She was cloth-coated and bent a cameo-like profile over the Chicago Sun-Times editorial page. And she was frowning. I suppose, Boyce thought, I should offer her the seat by the window.

He did.

The girl said suspiciously: "No thank you."

That was that for ten minutes.

Chuffing over the dreary west side he opened his own copy of the Sun-Times and buried himself in the misdeeds of the Republican-dominated Illinois legislature. Abruptly the girl said: "Are you from Chicago?"

"Yes," he said.

"Are you doing anything about that sort of thing?" She pointed to the exposé article in the newspaper.

"Well, there isn't much one person can—"

"That's where you're wrong. Let me tell you how the average person can do something about it. Who's the captain of your precinct?"

"Uh—I don't know."

"You're a Democrat, aren't you?" she demanded. That was because he had been reading the Sun-Times rather than the Tribune. Actually he wasn't so sure he was a Democrat.

"I suppose I am."

She took out a notebook. "Would you mind giving me your address?" Weakly, he did. She jotted and muttered: "That's Mr. McGavney's territory. Lived there long?"

"Ah—twelve years."

"Disgraceful!" she sputtered. "Mr. McGavney should be well acquainted with you by now and you with him. Somebody's going to hear about this, I promise you. These older men—they get lax."

It was going too far! "Look," he insisted, "don't you go getting anybody in trouble on my account! Maybe I'm not a Democrat and maybe

Mr. McGavney was perfectly right to stay away from me. Just please don't denounce him to anybody and say it's because of me."

She said implacably: "There must be discipline."

"I refuse to let you use my name in this thing. That's definite."

She said: "Very well. I'll use it for background only." She snapped her notebook shut and put it away. "Now," she went on, "you were asking what part the average person can take in politics."

The hell he was! Was he going to be stuck with this woman for two thousand miles?

"I, for instance, am fortunate enough to have a small income. I'm able to devote my full time to politics on the local level—the unglamorous local level. You can't be a prima donna down where I work; it's doorbell-ringing, handbill writing, patiently getting to know the people on your beat and persuading those who have to be persuaded, reminding the ones who get lazy about registration and voting. It's begging, too—a dollar here and a dollar there. We're the poor party, always have been. Now, you're obviously a professional man—"

"Assistant buyer. Floor coverings," he said.

"Yes, a professional or business man with a full day and many contacts. Have you thought of forming a Democratic caucus in your floor-coverings department?"

His eyes bulged at the thought. He would last maybe fifteen minutes after he was detected forming a Democratic caucus in his department. Just as long as it took to compute his severance pay. The same would go for anybody caught organizing a Republican caucus, or doing anything except what conduced to bigger and better sales of floor coverings. "I'm afraid that wouldn't be practicable," he said.

She wagged her head pityingly. "A victim of the climate of fear that has engulfed our country," she said. "You're a citizen of the world's greatest democracy and you're afraid to speak up in its behalf."

"I am not," he said, quite annoyed. "I simply think there's a time and place for politics. The time is not my boss' time and the place is not my boss' store."

A sleek, elderly porpoise-like dining car attendant came in from the vestibule and announced: "First call for luncheon, ladies and gentlemen. First call."

Thank God, thought Boyce. He got up and said: "I didn't have much breakfast getting away. I think I'll go to the diner." He realized with further annoyance that this young woman was somehow causing him to eat earlier than he cared to, to tell a lie about it, and to feel guilty all at the same time.

"I believe I'll freshen up and then have lunch myself," she said.

Mr. Cutler stood swaying, balanced on the balls of his feet, in the dining car vestibule. His responsibility was heady in him. Seniority at last had got him on a streamliner; only talent would keep him there. Anxiously he surveyed the dining car and noted that Table Seven, four seats, was about to be vacated by a couple and their half-grown children. And the surging mob behind him, growling for lunch, contained no parties of four.

The rulebook said simply: Seat like with like. Seat soldiers with soldiers, civilians with civilians. Negroes with Negroes, whites with whites. Women with women and men with men as far as possible. That was the out.

He turned and studied the waiting crowd in the vestibule, avoiding eyes and lifted fingers, and slowly composed his group for Table Seven.

A note of elegance. He beckoned a haughty, lovely, green-eyed, mink-coated, orchid-adorned woman of the world to him and admired her as she came. "Seat you in a moment, Miss," he said confidentially.

Now another lady. Not one who would challenge the first lady with a rival elegance, but somebody who would set it off. He beckoned a woman of perhaps thirty-two, wearing a good cloth coat over a good, slightly mannish grey suit. They'd have lots to talk about. "Seat you in a moment, Miss."

The young man with the brooding, intelligent look forced himself on Mr. Cutler. Well-dressed, but with something of the Bohemian about him—a writer or a newspaperman, perhaps. Mr. Cutler beckoned. "Seat you in a moment, sir."

The last choice was inevitable. The smallish fellow with the glasses who looked a little like Mr. Truman. He would be the indispensable, the Audience to the other three. Mr. Cutler beckoned. "Seat you in a moment, sir."

His timing was perfect. As the quartet was completed, the family at Table Seven rose and blundered down the aisle. "This way, please," said Mr. Cutler to his work of art, and seated them.

Back at his vantage-point in the vestibule he smiled for a moment at his arrangement. That was the psychology of it. They were calmly unfolding napkins, saying a tentative word or two, no hostility, no snooting of the cloth coat or envious glaring at the mink. Well, they were set for the trip, thank goodness. He would be worthy of the Golden Gate Express, Mr. Cutler vowed, or go down trying.

Boyce smiled crosswise over the table at Miss Lundberg. "Well, here we are again," he said, and hoped she wouldn't start talking politics. Directly across the table from him sat a young man who looked as if he might carry the conversational ball. "I hear we're going to have some snow," Boyce said to him.

The young man started and said: "That so? Uh, my name's Foreman. It looks as if we're going to eat together a few times."

"Samuel Boyce," the rug man told him. "And this is Miss Lundberg. We're in the same berth."

Miss Lundberg glared at him and the dark lovely person next to Boyce chuckled and said: "Indeed?"

The rug man began to explain unhappily what he meant, and they all wound up laughing.

Foreman said: "Don't I know you?" to the dark woman.

"You may have seen my picture," she said composedly. "I'm Mona Greer. I write."

"Of course! Thighs of the Wild Mare."

Joan Lundberg said: "Well! A celebrity at the same table with us. It could only happen in this republic—"

Boyce winced, ready for more of the political oratory, but the waiter saved them. By the time they had marked their choices on the menu Foreman was in charge. "I'm a newsman myself," he told Mona Greer.

"Did you see the morning Sun-Times?" Joan Lundberg asked. "About the tax scandals?"

"All taxes are scandalous," Mona Greer said firmly. "Especially mine. This is a business trip, for example, to promote my book. I shall list it as a business expense. And some time next spring the revenue people will start nagging and haggling about it, wanting to know whether I couldn't have taken an upper berth instead of a compartment and what proof I have that I tipped the maid five dollars. It will wind up with them disallowing about twenty-five percent of my claim and warning me not to let it happen again. And then in the spring of the following year the same thing will happen all over again." She had her eye on the Lundberg girl and forced her to smile sympathetically. What, she wondered, was that one wrapped up in? And mightn't it be interesting to unwrap her?

"Nothing like that in business," Boyce said, grateful that he could contribute. "I'm with Siegel's, the department store, and there's never any trouble over taxes. I have my little book, everything goes down in it and that's that."

The waiter swayed down the aisle, forearms balancing the trays, and beamed as he served them. "Yes, indeedy, folks," he said soothingly, as if they were children or fractious horses whom he must saddle. "Yes, indeedy," as he dealt them the dishes. "Gonna be big snow, folks," he said.

"The train won't be delayed, will it?" Boyce asked.

"Nossir, no indeedy. Nothing's gonna hold up the streamliner, folks. No indeedy. You all set now, folks?" And he beamed and was gone.

"There had better not be a holdup," Mona Greer said. "I'm on a split-second schedule. Autographing party, dinner party, cocktails—I feel like a freight car in the hands of the dispatcher." She began to dissect her brook trout delicately.

"Does your publisher line those things up?" Foreman asked. Something about the woman was intensely disagreeable. She had literally dragged the question from him, with a half-smile thrown his way just before her knife and fork—held in the European manner—started to probe the small bones and tender flesh. The question she forced him to ask lined them both up for any listeners: she the Author, he the Outsider with his respectful curiosity. But what listeners? Mr. Boyce? Miss Lundberg?

Mona Greer answered entertainingly, modestly but with sparkle. He barely listened, for obviously he was no longer needed; he was a straight man without any lines to speak. Unquestionably Miss Greer—or was it Mrs.?—was playing for Mr. Boyce and Miss Lundberg.

Joan Lundberg smiled back impulsively at serene Mona Greer. It would be nice to have her for a friend, she thought—

Boyce liked her too, and listened avidly to the exotic shoptalk of the publishing world. It was extremely interesting shoptalk and Mona Greer was an extremely interesting—and handsome—person. He liked the thought that he was dining with somebody whose name was known to millions—well, more likely thousands—and that she seemed to find him interesting too. He thought vaguely of her in bed—

There was a rough-house from the vestibule and everybody in the dining car craned or turned to see.

"Soldiers," Mona Greer said contemptuously.

A big hayseed in olive drab and a few campaign ribbons was yelling at the rather funny little man who had seated them: "Goddamn it, you already done passed us over three times! Ain't we supposed to be good enough to eat with the civilians?"

The funny little man tried to soothe him and three or four muttering G.I.'s with him. With a flash of well-cut, well-pressed slacks and blouse, a young officer strode down the aisle to the vestibule, still carrying his napkin.

"Stop your yelling, soldier!" he snapped at the hayseed. "It's a good damn thing there isn't a pair of train M.P.'s aboard. Now what's the beef here?"

"Lieutenant," the hayseed said, with outrage and self-pity in his voice, "this man done passed us over three times and he was just fixing to do it again. We get just as hungry as civilians and time we get to Alaska we're gonna be hungrier—"

"Don't talk about troop movements," the officer said fiercely. "How long have you been in the Army anyway? Conductor, you didn't do anything like that, did you?"

The funny little man began an involved story about rules and the lieutenant cut him off. "There," he said to the G.I.'s. "Nobody was discriminating. You're hungry and jumpy and you imagined it. Just keep your shirts on and you'll get a seat."

He turned and strode back down the aisle to his interrupted luncheon, a tanned, fit, trim, tailored, smug young man with bright silver bars on his shoulders, very pleased with himself and the world in which he could tell them off and they couldn't tell him off.

"I'd like," Foreman said quietly, "to spit right in his eye."

Mona Greer said: "I take it you were an enlisted man," and smiled at Joan Lundberg and Boyce with her eyes. The strange enmity there again enraged him. It flashed through his mind to be savagely witty at her expense—but he'd come off second-best in any exchange. The great Mona Greer was no latter-day Dorothy Parker, but she undoubtedly could make a monkey out of him. He looked down at his minute steak, cut off a piece and chewed it tastelessly. The cards were stacked; why try?

Boyce said: "I suppose I was lucky. Too young for the first and too old for the second. If you call it luck."

"Men," Mona Greer smiled at Joan Lundberg. "'If you call it luck.' I have never met a man who didn't feel that messy compulsion to kick somebody's teeth in, get his own arm broken and then stoutly maintain that he had a perfectly wonderful time."

Joan laughed delightedly. "Perfectly true, Miss Greer," she said. "In politics, which I know a little about, it's the women workers who try to make deals first. The men want a knockdown, drag-out fight and when they can get what they want by a horse-trade they resent it."

Foreman looked up suddenly. The lineup now was clear. The two women were smiling with amused condescension at the two men. Mona Greer had cut out first him and then Boyce; she was making her play for Miss Lundberg. Boyce didn't know what was going on; it was a good joke, amusing table talk, and he didn't mind being the butt of a good joke.

The lieutenant, still proud of himself, followed a slim red-headed girl down the aisle. Mona Greer touched his sleeve as he passed. "Lieutenant?"

He turned courteously and said: "Ma'am?"

"Lieutenant, I just wanted to say that I admired the way you quelled the near-riot. I think you were a perfect horse's ass."

"Why, it's very kind of you, ma'am—" the lieutenant began. Then his face went very dark, and he turned and strode on.

Joan Lundberg gasped, and Boyce strangled down a guffaw of surprise. "Was that right, Mr. Foreman?" Mona Greer asked. "Or should I have spat in his eye?"

"You did very well, Miss Greer," Foreman said, and again the words had been dragged from him. She would have been a great confidence woman. Struggle as he might, he couldn't break out of the framework of the little drama she had composed for them all and in which they were all playing their parts. Mona the leading lady. Joan the admiring ingenue. Boyce the low comic. Foreman the ineffectual heavy. No hero, you'll notice; not in Mona's little script. Maybe its title was Anything They Can Do We Can Do Better.

Joan Lundberg spoke her lines: "Miss Greer, why on earth did you say that?"

"Oh, he looked so bloody smug I couldn't stand it. Mr. Foreman couldn't stand it either, but the iron discipline of the Old Army inhibited him. The Army's gone to hell, hasn't it, Mr. Foreman?"

It was a dazzling jab that caught him flat-footed. Suddenly he was required to make a joking reply from the pretended viewpoint of a thirty-year man. Startled, all he could say was, after a lame pause: "So they tell me." Mona's look gave him a hint of arch sympathy. Too bad you're so dumb; we'll try not to notice it.

The waiter brought their coffee.

"You nice people," Mona Greer smiled at them, "will you all come and have cocktails at six with me in my compartment? I've conscientiously brought my typewriter and I'm afraid I'll get some work done if I don't rigorously avoid it."

"Why, I'd love to," Joan Lundberg said, and she meant it. Miss Greer—Mona—was turning out to be a very delightful person to know.

"Sure; thanks!" Boyce said, dazzled.

"Delighted," Foreman said, after a pause. The woman was detestable, but his acceptance was in the script she had written for them. According to the script they were witty, civilized people who held small cocktail parties and accepted invitations to them. He couldn't back out without a churlish explanation, loss of face, looks of wonder from the others.

They paid their checks and rose, and filed down the aisle of the swaying diner. Their departure was the signal for the seating of the four disgruntled G.I.'s, who were still sulking.

CHAPTER IX

SNOW

Willie Harris, station engineer at KLTG Denver, and Max Murphy, announcer, were drinking their lunch in the bar of the Hotel Schuyler.

"—so I said to him, 'sonny, we're proud and grateful that you decided to offer us your services. And just as soon as we're in the market for a half-baked youngster with a journalism degree and delusions of grandeur, we'll let you know.' Sixty-five a week he wanted, for God's sake!"

Harris haw-hawed. Murphy looked at his expensive announcer's watch in sudden alarm. "Jesus," he said. "Three minutes and twenty seconds to the noon newscast!" He streaked from the bar and upstairs to the studio, no time for the elevators. He arrived winded but with fifteen seconds to catch his breath before the mike.

The double door from the newsroom opened and one of the boys laid the script on the table before him. On top of it was a bulletin torn direct from one of the teletypes.

Murphy took a deep breath and said: "This is the twelve o'clock news. First, a bulletin from the wires of the Associated Press. Denver—the United States Weather Bureau here has just warned that the developing snowstorm over the Rockies may be the worst so far this winter—possibly in many winters. Snow and sub-zero temperatures may well combine to cause unprecedented damage to livestock on winter range and disruption of transportation and communication ..."

He could read it without bothering to think. Same old stuff, everybody trying to get into the act. He could taste the last rye-with-beer-chaser, and wondered why he—why so many radio people drank like fishes. Maybe because so many stations were in hotels...

"...railroad officials said there is no cause for alarm and that delays will be only trifling. They admitted that snowplows are being held ready in case of...

CHAPTER X

UPPER AND LOWER BERTHS

Boyce stood aside for Joan to slip in and take the seat by the window.

"Do you think," she asked abruptly, "that she meant it?"

Boyce wondered for a wild moment whether they were back on politics, and if "she" was Eleanor Roosevelt. Then he caught on. Mona Greer's cocktail party, of course.

"Why, yes," he said. "Do you think she might have been kidding?"

"It suddenly crossed my mind. Why should she be interested in us? Why should she bother with us at all? She knows all kinds of people. Writers, artists."

"That fellow, Foreman—a newspaperman. They lead interesting lives." She snorted.

"I'm wrong?" he asked.

"Lord, yes. I was a newspaperwoman. Deadly, dull routine. Maybe fifty or a hundred newspapermen in the country get to do interesting work, write about what they want, when they want. But by then they're sixty years old. The rest are just people with a little bag of tricks any twelve-year-old could pick up in a month. Maybe the way things are going, they'll have machines to do reporting and rewrite in another twenty years."

"How could that be?" he asked seriously.

She laughed. "I was joking. But really, there are only a few dozen news stories. The only real difference between one robbery and another is how the blanks are filled in. Now, creative writing ..." She fell into a silence.

"Like Miss Greer," he supplied. It was getting interesting. The girl was more than a humorless political fanatic.

"Yes," she said. And: "I still don't understand it."

"These writers," said Boyce. "Maybe she's studying us. For her next book. I hear they do that. They don't just copy a person cold, but they take one thing from one person and another thing from another and before you know it, they have a character. Maybe that's what she's up to."

"She doesn't write about people like us. I've heard of her book. She writes about artists and sculptors and musicians. In places like Tangiers and Fire Island and Capri."

"Where's Fire Island? I never heard of it."

"Frankly, neither have I. But every review I read of her book seemed to make a point of mentioning it. I guess it's a very, very sophisticated resort that we rabble wouldn't know about."

"She is sophisticated," he agreed. "I've sold carpets to some very, very wealthy people—but she's different. She must be the kind that goes to one of those decorator places and gets rooked. Wouldn't be seen in any place as common as a first-rate department store."

She laughed with him; it made him feel good. And then, defending her new friend Mona against her new friend Boyce, she argued: "But maybe she sees more in us than we know we have in us. For instance, I'm a pianist and a good one. Maybe a writer can tell."

"Pianist too? You're a very remarkable young lady!"

"I never did anything serious with it; I'm not good enough for that—not nowadays, with the competition what it is. And I don't have a piano where I am—you're not Swedish, are you?"

"No; not a bit."

And then Joan found herself telling him about the damned prying Nilsens, making it a funny story, a battle of wits between her and them in which privacy was the prize. Then she noticed that her hands were shaking and her voice was too shrill. She put her hands on her knees and pressed them there; the shaking stopped. She concluded flatly: "So you see, I'm really going to have to move out of there the first chance I get."

Such a thought had never crossed her mind before. The place was clean and convenient and the spying was a minor nuisance; she had nothing to hide from the Nilsens or anybody. And yet she had just told this man as a foregone conclusion that she was moving out.

"Sometimes," said Boyce, "I get that feeling myself. Times when I know I've taken absolutely as much as I can stand."

"What do you do then? Ah—drink?"

He shrugged. "No. I just go on standing it. You can't run away from a good job. Where do you work, Miss Lundberg?"

She had long ago perfected a little routine for calming people staggered by the fact that she didn't have to work, that she had an independent income. "There's a little trust fund that keeps me going," she said. "If I ever want to buy something new I get a job somewhere until I've saved up enough." She had actually had to do it once only, when she thought she wanted a car, changed her mind when she got it and turned it back to the dealer in a week.

At this point most people pretended that they understood perfectly; that they knew dozens of people situated exactly like her; that only some accident or other had prevented them from having a little trust fund that kept them going. But Boyce said wonderingly: "I never met anybody before who didn't have to work. What's it like?"

She thought a long minute before answering. "I suppose," she said slowly, "I'm freer this way. I can spend my time on what's important, which to my mind is politics. There are so very few of us, so much to be done. I put in a ten-hour day. During campaigns, more. What's it like? I don't really know; I've never had to work. I suppose my father worked hard enough for two, so here I am with a check once a month from the Midland Trust people."

He had worked hard, her father. Society portrait painter; wit, bon vivant, indefatigable Don Juan, fountain of vitality and charm until the last horrible days. He had worked hard, her damnably interesting, damnably brilliant father, whose brilliance had made her childhood a hell on earth...

She said dryly: "He gave me an education, which is more than most people get, and some money, which is a lot more than most people get. I suppose he was all right." She noticed that her hands were trembling again, and again she pressed them against her knees.

Boyce watched her and knew suddenly that she was in terror, of what he could not guess. And he would have given the world to take her in his arms and comfort her fear... he thought of the last woman he had taken in his arms. That tramp at the dance hall. That disgusting tramp who knew exactly what she wanted and how to get it. That tramp who was not unlike his wife, who also knew what and how. The pair of them utterly unlike this girl beside him, this girl who was, he thought, very much like himself.

Joan Lundberg said: "About Miss Greer. I suppose I should try and sell her on good government. Maybe she could make it the theme of her next book—"

They both paused and thought and laughed at the idea. Laughed rather shakily.

"Not her," Boyce said emphatically.

"Well, why not?" Joan demanded. "It's everybody's business; why not hers? She has talent, she can reach thousands of people. I really ought to try." She stared for a moment at the blurred and flying landscape through the window. "But I won't," she said. "I'm on vacation—at least while I'm on the train."

"Look," Boyce pointed. "Snow!"

It was a white flurry that seemed to move horizontally because of the speed of the train.

"I feel mixed up," Joan Lundberg said. "Excuse me, please." She slid past Boyce and went to the ladies' room at the end of the car, frozen-faced as a lady should be on such an errand. Her discontent, her bewilderment, the feeling that something long knotted-up was going to come loose, usually meant one thing, which happened every twenty-eight days.

In the dressing room she fished through her handbag and found the little card with an insurance company's name and a calendar for the year printed on it. She checked the date last circled: thirteen days ago. She was not coming sick, no matter how much it felt like it.

A woman smoking on one of the leather seats noticed the card, guessed at it, and cleared her throat to ask: "Is anything wrong? Can I lend you anything?"

Joan looked at her and found her young, fat and ruddy.

"No," she told her. "Thanks very much. I just feel a little under the weather. Maybe I'm carsick."

The fat girl said: "Want to stretch out here? The Pullman maid's got aspirin. Uh, maybe you could use a drink?" Shyly she produced a dark pint bottle which had been wedged between her meaty thigh and the wall of the car. "Cognac. The best." She held out the bottle and Joan distractedly took it. Hadn't she just said it was a vacation, at least while she was on the train? Snow swirled past the window.

"Thanks," she said. "Maybe it will make me feel better." She took one of the little rinsing cups from the wall dispenser and poured it half-full, balancing against the sway of the car, and gulped it down.

"No wash," the fat girl commented. "I don't bother myself."

Joan nodded, her throat on fire, and handed back the bottle. She had to sit down.

"Bet you don't know where I come from," the fat girl said, pouring herself a drink in a paper cup and wedging the bottle back into hiding. "The Galapagos Islands. I'll bet you don't know where they are."

"Off the western coast of South America," Joan said. Her voice sounded very clear and distant to her. "Turtles."

"Good for you!" her friend said. "Everybody knows about the turtles but I bet you're the only person on the Continent that knows what ocean they're in. People tell me India, China, Siberia, the Mediterranean. You a schoolteacher?"

"No. I'm a—I don't know. I really don't know." Joan began to cry, sitting straight upright with her hands folded in her lap.

"For God's sake," the girl said. She got up and went to the sink, and Joan dimly saw that she was not only fat but pregnant, and began to cry harder.

"Here," the girl said, giving her another of the paper cups. "Should I try to scare up a doctor for you?"

Joan gulped the cupful—more cognac, with water. The thin, fiery spirit curled warmly in her stomach and after a moment she felt less alone, less knotted-up and about to come loose and she could stop crying with loneliness and apprehension.

Her voice, though, still shook when she said: "I think I'll be all right. Feels like cramps—I mean I'm depressed like with cramps—only nothing's going on." She wiped her eyes and blew her nose with Kleenex which somehow had got into her hand.

"If it was last month I could understand that," the girl said. "I don't go in for astrology or bunk like that, but I notice my period's always a few days off schedule around the summer solstice. Of course," she said, looking down on her bulging abdomen with wry pride, "it hasn't happened lately."

"When's the baby due?" Joan asked eagerly.

"About a month, I guess."

"You left the—the Galapagos Islands to have it?"

"My friend, I was kicked out of the Galapagos Islands to have it. My loving parents thought the native boys would talk." She held out her left hand. There was no ring on the third finger. "I am a remittance woman."

"Oh."

"You're very good," the fat girl grinned. "You know what ocean the Galapagos Islands are in and you don't ask me who the father is and what I'm going to do."

"Really," Joan began faintly, and then stopped. It was like something that would happen on the detestable, pinko south side. It was the kind of encounter which one feared and avoided. But, astonishingly, this woman—this loose-moraled, unreticent, undoubtedly pinko person—was a nice person who had helped her. Joan held tight, tight, fearing she would cry again.

A slim, lovely red-headed girl—Joan knew her; she had lunched with the lieutenant Mona Greer insulted—swept in between the dusty curtains and yanked open one of the booth doors as though there were no possibility of it being locked against her entrance. It clicked behind her, arrogantly.

The fat girl grinned at the door and muttered: "Boston. She joy-pops."

"I—I beg your pardon?"

"Joy-pops. Takes narcotics."

"How could you possibly know that?" protested Joan.

"Everybody uses it where I come from. The field hands are Peruvians, and coca's the biggest industry in Peru."

"You must be teasing me. If everybody took cocaine no work would get done, they'd all get sick—it's impossible," Joan smiled. She wouldn't be taken in by travellers' tales.

"That's all you know about it, my friend," said the girl good-humoredly. "Cocaine's bad stuff. It's white man stuff. But coca leaf—well, the Indians have been taking it for at least four thousand years. And they still call it 'gift of God'."

"But dope's bad," Joan said.

"Yes?" asked the fat girl, lighting a cigarette. "You like music? Opera?"

"I used to go to the Chicago Opera. What's—?"

"You know about the golden age of opera forty-fifty years ago? When great singers were a dime a dozen?"

"Yes, of course."

"They did it on coca, my friend. A smart Corsican named Angelo Mariani put out Mariani's Vin Coca—good wine with coca leaves steeping in it. It was popular with singers, and that's where the golden age of opera came from. It gave them endurance and skill, the way it gives Peruvian miners and porters endurance and skill. The golden age of opera ended when the French government outlawed Vin Coca because it was cutting into champagne sales."

The girl didn't seem to be kidding and she did seem to be terrifyingly well-informed. "But dope," Joan said helplessly.

"Anything's good if you use it right. Anything's bad if you use it wrong. Like that one." She jerked her chin at the closed booth door.

"You know a great deal."

"My friend, you too would know a great deal if you were a lonesome fat girl on a godforsaken island with a good library on the estancia and the ground rules didn't let you play with Americanos del Sur." She looked down at her abdomen with the same wry smile. "But I did," she grinned.

"You mean—with a native?"

She should despise her, Joan knew. Everybody knew that the pinkos wanted intermarriage, that they held it out to catch the Negro vote that should belong forever to the Democrats who gave them F.D.R. This experience should be embarrassing and ugly—but she wanted to giggle instead at the thought of the parents being outwitted and outraged. This was most upsetting.

"I don't recommend it for anybody else," the fat girl said. "I liked them. They were nice guys. They all claimed they were descended from the Inca kings, which was the bunk. Prescott proves it in Conquest of Mexico and Peru. But they couldn't read Prescott and believed it, so what difference did it make? They were all nice guys."

"Excuse me," Joan said. "I don't mean to pry. But I want to know. Since you're going to have a baby. Shouldn't you try to lose weight? And about the drinking. Really, I'm not trying to push you around." Perhaps the girl didn't know about the dangers of overweight to the mother during delivery. Perhaps she might be able to help her.

"That's all right," the girl said. "Some impressive medical talent agrees that I won't live through it."

"But," Joan said wildly after a long pause, "that can't be true. Caesarians—"

"A Caesarian," the girl said. "It doesn't sound bad. 'Caesarian section.' But it sounds mighty bad if you call it poisoning me until I almost die but not quite—that's the general anaesthetic—and then cutting me open clear to the uterus, yanking the baby out and sewing me up again. They tell me my heart won't take it."

The red-headed girl came out of the booth, looked at them and asked in a brittle, finishing-school voice: "May I join the hen party?" Joan noted that the pupils of her eyes were contracted to pin-points. So some of it was true, then.

"Please do," the fat girl said. "We were talking about life."

"Splendid," the red-headed girl said. "Mostly my husband talks about death. He's going to manage a supply depot on a certain Asiatic island which must be nameless because of security requirements. He's scared out of his wits, God love him." She lit a cigarette.

"He woke me up couple of nights ago at three-thirty. Not for anything interesting, mind you. He'd been lying there and thinking. If the balloon goes up, he tells me, he wants me to wait for him. He will return."

"What balloon is this?" asked the pregnant girl.

"Civilians! Service people don't say 'If World War Three starts'. They say 'If the balloon goes up.' Don't ask me why; that's just the jargon. Anyway, he has it all figured out. They'll invade the island with a fleet of junks. The first wave of troops will be fanatics, specially trained, kill-crazy. His duty, he says, is to stay out of the hands of the assault wave of troops; they'll butcher everybody in uniform. After the island's taken and they begin to organize, he'll come down out of the hills and surrender himself to a commissioned officer, the higher the better. They'll ship him to the mainland, they'll march him to a prison camp in the interior, and then he'll be okay if he lasts out the march. That, he says, depends on the weather. The point is, when he's reported missing in action, I'm not to jump to any conclusions and start messing around. He'll take care of himself and he'll be back."

"So there's going to be another war," the pregnant girl said.

"Certainly not," Joan said sharply. "The policy of containment—"

The red-headed girl laughed sharply. "Civilians!" she said again. "What I wouldn't give to be a civilian again. The war is on for us service people; we're just waiting for it to hit the headlines. Rick's been a Pentagon Indian for the past eighteen months, on a ten-hour, six-day week. And that doesn't mean Sundays off, either. They work a swing-shift. And we've been watching our friends getting their troop-duty assignments one by one. Oh, those farewell parties. Germany's good duty, lots of housing and servants, and there you are right on the front line—"

"When the balloon goes up," said Joan.

"Yes. England's good duty too. Afternoon tea and all that. And then one day six medium-size atomic bombs blow up six English ports and the English starve to death in a few months, and you starve with them unless you're air-lifted back to the States. Oh, England's swell duty. But Asia. Kids, that's it. They hate our living guts, every last brown-skinned brother out there. The place not to be when the balloon goes up is Asia. So naturally that's where they're sending Rick."

"But we have firm friends in Asia," Joan said. "The Philippines. Japan. I watch the international situation—"

"Good," said the red-headed girl. "You do that. Service wives don't watch the international situation; we watch the little back-page items. Like what happened the day after the Japanese got back their sovereignty. They celebrated by arresting about fifty G.I.'s and officers for being drunk and disorderly. We knew one of the officers and we knew he never took a drink in his life. And Rick—he'll have to fly to get to the island. Maybe a Mig will knock his transport down on general principles and if they pick him up he'll be tried as a spy. You know what they do to them; maybe he'll wind up admitting he's a spy. You know what they do to them."

"Lot of if's and maybe's in that," the pregnant girl said wryly. Joan knew she was thinking about her own case, about which there seemed to be no if's or maybe's at all.

"It's a bore, isn't it?" the red-headed girl asked brightly. "Well, where are you girls headed?"

"National Conference of Democratic Women's Clubs in San Francisco," said Joan. "I'm delegate from the Scandia Club in Chicago."

"That's interesting. Will you give the ladies a message from me?"

"Uh—of course."

"Tell 'em they can do a few things for me. Tell 'em Rick's four years at the Academy ought to be computed as active service for pay and longevity, will you? Tell 'em there ought to be some kind of civilian medical care available for dependents where there aren't service facilities. Tell 'em to pass the Substandard Housing Act so service people won't get swindled by trailer camps and tourist courts. Tell 'em—oh, just tell them to stop treating the Regulars like stepchildren."

"I'll try," said Joan.

"You think I'm a spoiled brat, don't you?"

There was a long silence. The red-headed girl got up and dropped her cigarette. "I'm sorry I intruded," she said, quite tonelessly, and swept through the curtains.

"Hell," the fat girl said, angry with herself. "Now we've hurt her feelings. I'm sorry about that."

"She shouldn't have talked that way about her husband."

"She talked the way she had to."

Two middle-aged women came in, talking, and went into the booths. They carried on their conversation, indistinctly, from booth to booth.

"I think I'll get back to my seat," Joan said. "It's been nice talking to you. I hope I'll see you again."

Good heavens, it had been nice talking to her, she marveled as she swayed down the aisle to her seat. And oddly, with this thought came another thought: that it was really not very nice talking to Mona Greer, for all her fame and wit and chic. Which was absurd. Of course it was nice talking to Mona Greer; anybody who was famous, witty and chic must be nice to talk to and listen to.

She thought Boyce's eyebrows went up a little as she slid past him to the window seat. The snow was now a white muslin sheet hung against the window. You could see telegraph poles, ghosts of telegraph poles, flashing past but nothing more.

"If you smell liquor on my breath," she told Boyce a little tartly, "it's because I didn't feel well and a woman in the rest room happened to offer me some brandy."

"I wish," Boyce said disconsolately, "you'd brought some for me. I've just been sitting here watching the snow and feeling so blue I could bawl. And it's stupid. I'm in the prime of life, I've got a fair career cut out, I've got a good wife. Dr. Anthony, what's my problem?" They laughed at the oldie, briefly and artificially.

"No children?" Joan asked.

There was a look of pain on his face, but his voice was cheerful enough—cheerful and phony as a square grape. "No; we don't want them. We're too selfish, I guess. Why raise a family in times like these."

Joan almost began a furious protest, but choked it off before it started. He was lying. He wanted children; he wasn't selfish; he wanted to raise a family in times like these or any other times.

"May I see her picture?" she asked. It was a safe guess; he pulled his wallet from his left hip pocket and showed her the inevitable picture. It was a reduction of a, say, fifteen-dollar Michigan Boulevard photographer's studio portrait. The woman was a brunette, small-eyed, slightly pudgy-nosed. Her lips were curved in a half-smile and her lips were lowered invitingly. A housewife-whore, at least by virtue of the fifteen-dollar Michigan Boulevard studio.

"Thanks. She's pretty," Joan said.

"You're prettier," Boyce told her, not looking at her.

"You shouldn't talk like that," she said sharply.

"All right," he said. "I won't. Usually I don't."

It was embarrassing. He stared at his toes and she stared through the window, or tried to. There was nothing to see but the zipping wraiths of telephone poles, and they were getting harder to see. The snow was becoming heavier. They were heading west, and it was not yet dusk.

Of course he shouldn't have talked like that. Whatever faults the woman had, she was his wife. Joan wondered what the fat girl from the Galapagos Islands would have to say about that. After she had punished him with a few more minutes of stony silence she would tell him about her—not the intimate stuff. That wasn't any man's business.

But when she turned to him after five minutes—judged by a furtive glance at her wrist watch—he had dozed off.

Damn him! she thought.

He looked small, defenseless and mousier than ever, and very tired. Apparently one of his wife's faults was addiction to canned goods and the delicatessen. He was a man suffering from the fatigue of years on an unbalanced diet, and the lines in his face spoke of other strains: unexpressed angers, appetites denied.

She could take better care of a man than that. And any woman who didn't want children was a fool and didn't deserve a husband.

But of course whatever faults she had, she was his wife.

CHAPTER XI

SNOW

Daniel Menafee, his left hand on the dead man's button and his right on the throttle of the giant twin diesel-electric locomotive, hummed to himself as the train flashed proudly past the town of Alhambra. He could read the station sign in spite of the thickening snow.

He glanced at the clock, though it was hardly necessary. He was on schedule to the second. The long list of towns the train would flash past unrolled in his mind without an effort, together with the times of departure. Why, the snow meant nothing to the thundering monster he controlled with his fingertips!

His "fireman" asked: "Spell you, Dan?"

Daniel Menafee grunted once for "no." Sometimes he had to be spelled, when his bladder was ready to burst, but until then he didn't like to turn over this beautiful monster to any other hands.

Wenatchi flashed past.

This time he couldn't read the station sign.

CHAPTER XII

COMPARTMENT

Mona Greer lay in the dark on the floor of her compartment, feeling the jar of the roadbed through her hips and shoulders. It distracted her. This was supposed to be two hours of utter relaxation during the afternoon—a practice said to have prolonged the life and looks of Lady Mendl and other European beauties. Mona had been faithfully lying on the floor for two hours in the dark daily for some months now. It was rather silly, it cut into her day and one could never be sure of whether it worked, but something had to be done. Mona Greer was growing old and knew it.

She got up from the floor and stretched out on one of the two lowers in her compartment. It was better. She couldn't clear her mind of random thoughts because of the jolting, but she could feel her muscles go soft one by one, the tautness in her felt relaxing, her leg muscles and thigh muscles turning limp...

But thoughts still came crowding in. She had, thank God, a few good years left whether this absurd business worked or not. More and more her habitat would become candlelit cafes; more and more of her time she would spend in Europe. Never, she told herself passionately, never would she become a Maggie Buckle, fat and shrieking, getting her vicarious kicks from the goings-on of the young folks. And never, by God, never, would she buy it. She had money; that's what husbands are for; but no young tart would ever get a nickel of it from her. That would be an essential denial of what she stood for. Robert Graves, one of the few men alive who understood women, wrote: "...to overpower by the perfumed sweetness of her presence ..." That was essential. The climactic explosions through the flesh were only part of it. "...to overpower by the perfumed sweetness of her presence ..."; to feel the submission she commanded, to savor the climax and then to confirm her mastery of the pleasure-instrument by breaking her and throwing her away with a few choice words of revelation or a crack of one's palm across a tear-wet face. She liked them to cry, she thought lazily; it set off one's own relaxation in higher relief. Without pain there could be no pleasure, of course, since they are opposites. There, darling! By irrefutable logic you confirm the truth of what you know by instinct. She smiled in the dark, not knowing that the smile was a crazy, teeth-baring, raging grin of predatory hatred.

Her little traveling clock sounded its alarm and she swung from the berth and snapped up the shades. Snow: sheets of it. A freak of the wind blasted a clear tunnel through the falling white for a moment and she saw rolling cornland blanketed for hundreds of yards before the curtain dropped again.

Humming scraps of Debussy, she selected her wardrobe. Nothing would happen tonight with that wrapped-up, tense blonde girl Joan Lundberg, but it was as well to feel secure. She chose a satin-and-lace strapless black corselet and smilingly mouthed the Victorian euphemism: invincible bastion of honor. It hung from her hands, a rectangle of flimsy cloth, puckered and pocketed into shapelessness. The shapelessness startlingly conformed to her body as she held it against her. With pretty concentration, her arms behind her worked the hooks and eyes of honor's invincible bastion.

The old frauds had probably known quite well that there are men and women, hundreds of thousands of them, who are driven especially crazy by corsets as some are by fancy high heels, others long hair and still others actually go for rubber raincoats in this mad world.

She hesitated between brown and black nylons and chose the black, thinking: the touch of bitchery and witchery, but not overdone. Over it all, the Little Black Dress that would look exactly that to the men, and which the girl would instantly know cost four hundred and fifty dollars in Paris. A bizarre variation in gold of one of those British regimental badges, a piece of Greenwich Village slop her publisher had given her, caught the neckline and led the eye to speculate on the valley between her firm breasts.

She tied on a prosaic bib and began the minute preparation of her face. She did not finish a second too soon. At a knock on the door she whisked the bib off and out of sight. She could not call: "Who is it?" She had to open the door smiling, to deny that anything untoward could ever happen to her, that any situation could arise that she did not dominate.

It was Foreman, alone. "Am I early?" he asked.

She glanced at the traveling clock and said: "Exactly seven and one-half minutes, Mr. Foreman. Come in; I was dying of boredom. Tell me all about the fascinating life you musicians lead."

"Newspapermen," he said.

"Of course. I knew it was one of the major arts. You're an—an entertainment columnist, I think you said?"

"I didn't say. I'm a wire-service man. You get to do everything on the wire services. I've covered executions, I've had a column reviewing kiddies, phonograph records, I've been a basketball dopester. Right now I'm being a junior-type executive on my way to set up a San Francisco news bureau."

"Mr. Foreman," she said, "how are wire-service men at mixing drinks? An enemy of mine once gave me a thing called a Port-Ur-Bar and my New England conscience won't let me throw it away." She displayed the leather monstrosity, a suitcase outwardly and a compact little bar inside: tools, glassware for four, scotch, rye, gin, vermouth and brandy. "Ring for ice, and we have it made."

He rang, and told the porter.

"You travel in style," he said.

"Isn't it disgusting, Mr. Foreman? To like nice things and be able to afford them? I'm thinking of sharing my bounty. Perhaps Miss Lundberg, if tactfully approached, could be persuaded to move in with me. I don't like to see a pretty girl traveling in an upper berth like a paper-box salesman."

"Can you do that?" he asked evenly. "Arrange it with the conductor?"

"Oh, yes. I've done it before."

Now was the time, Foreman thought, to speak. And say—what? Lady, you're a Lesbian? Lady, leave that sweet innocent kid alone or I will have you put off the train? Quite impossible. Mona Greer's little playlet didn't have room in it for such lines. Nobody knew whether she was a Lesbian or not. Nobody could put her off the train. Nobody could stop her from doing such a generous and disinterested thing as offering one of her three spare berths to a nice girl traveling alone.

The ineffectual heavy spoke his lines: "What'll I mix?"

"For me, a bucket of four-to-one martinis. And I take my martinis seriously, Mr. Foreman. They are the Doric Order of cocktails. You must pour the booze on the ice and stir gently or nothing can save you. The last wire service man who mixed martinis for me dropped the ice in the booze. He was about to shake them instead of stirring when I went for him with the paring knife and had his left eye out."

"I heard about that," Foreman said. "Old Blinky Kaplan. His friends got him onto the Herald-American; he does a column three times a week reviewing the popcorn in the second run movie houses."

"You get to do everything on a Hearst paper," Mona said soberly, and they laughed.

What the hell, Foreman thought, remembering the ancient Chinese advice to a young lady about to be raped: relax and enjoy yourself. She was kind of nasty but she had brains and charm, the way a lot of queers do. You don't go out of your way to meet them, but if you're half-way civilized you don't slug them and walk away indignantly either. You take them as people with problems of their own and you relax and enjoy yourself if possible. And maybe he had this figured out wrong.

"What's the Ionic Order of cocktails, Miss Greer?" he asked.

"The three-in-ones: sidecars, stingers, alexanders."

"And the Corinthian Order?"

"The old fashioned, rightly known as 'whisky and garbage.'"

"We agree on cocktails, if on nothing else."

The ice arrived, in a bowl with tongs. Foreman tipped a quarter and was carefully mixing four-to-one martinis when Joan Lundberg and Boyce arrived. The first dinner chimes were echoing through the car.

Something happened then. The barglass sloshed wildly in Foreman's hands as he struggled for balance. Mona Greer was flung back into a berth, displaying a length of silk-clad leg to the thigh. Boyce and Joan clutched at each other and cannoned together into the compartment. They heard the dinner chimes crash to the corridor floor outside with a great jangle. And then everything went on as before while they picked themselves up and Foreman mopped martini from the lapel of his jacket.

The pullman porter's head popped into the open door. "Everything all right in here, folks?" he asked soothingly.

"So it seems," Mona told him. "What was that?"

"My guess, ma'am, the engineer reduced speed when he saw a snowdrift across the track. We take snowdrifts slow. Thank you, ma'am." He was gone.

"We'll be late," Mona said angrily. "I knew it. Stop playing with that booze, Foreman. Pour for a thirsty lady."

Foreman poured a brimming glass and passed it to her, trying not to grin. Sudden pneumatic brakes were something she couldn't handle. Perhaps there were other things.

"Martinis?" he asked Joan and Boyce.

"Whew. Yes, please," the rug man said. "I hope they ring a bell before they do that the next time. I'm awfully sorry I grabbed you, Joan."

Mona Greer raised her brows at the name. The girl didn't notice. "That's all right," she said a little shakily. "I grabbed you too." And to Foreman: "I'd better not have any. I wasn't feeling well after lunch and somebody gave me some brandy."

"Quite right, little one," Mona Greer said. "Stick with what you start with." She herself neatly poured a pony of brandy and put it into Joan's hand. Foreman, filling two more cocktail glasses, admired the deftness of it.

Mona raised her glass and said: "I give you Cyrus Field, by whose engineering genius and vision the broad Atlantic is now spanned with a telegraphic cable."

"Hear-hear!" said Foreman warmly. Boyce looked bewildered, but drank dutifully with the rest of them.

Foreman cleared his throat modestly and said: "I should like to toast a little-known hero of American industry. Ladies and gentleman, I give you the plant numbers-runner."

Boyce finally got it, and grinned happily. Foreman gravely refilled the three cocktail glasses and Mona made for the brandy flask.

"No," Joan laughed. "Really, I'll fall on my face."

"Little one, logic forces me to point out that you did fall on your face a minute ago and no harm was done. Besides, Mr. Boyce is going to give the next toast." Joan laughed and yielded.

Boyce stood with his glass poised and a frown of concentration on his face for long seconds and then declared: "Ladies and gentlemen, this occasion cannot pass without us paying honor to one of the nation's leading sonsa-bitches in the great field of retail merchandising. I give you Mr. Gottfried Oberholtzer, my boss."

Joan giggled and said: "It's my turn, isn't it? Um… Madame Chairlady, members, guests, parents, children, friends, enemies and visitors—I rise on a point of personal privilege to put in nomination—no, to name a man who combines the dignity of Washington, the tenderness of Jefferson, the clemency of Adams, the piety of Lincoln, the modesty of McClellan and the statesmanship of Bugs Bunny. Ladies and Gentlemen, I give you Louis Pasteur, played by Paul Muni."

They said: "Hear-hear!" and drank.

"I know when I'm licked, little one," Mona said. "I'm out of my class when there's a politician present."

"'Party worker' is a nicer way to put it, Miss Greer," Joan said primly.

"Call me Mona, little one. Anybody who can make one of those 'a man who' speeches on an empty stomach I am proud to have for a friend."

There was a diffident knock on the door. Annoyed, Mona rose and opened it.

A well-dressed lantern-jawed fellow said: "I'm awfully sorry to have disturbed you if everything's all right. I'm Dr. Groves. I know the porter checked, but I thought I ought to ask if anybody got hurt in that bump. Are you all okay in here?"

"Yes, and thanks very much, doctor. You're being very conscientious, I'm sure."

"With the help of Providence, ma'am," he said as they both started to turn. The word galvanized her. "Doctor!" she said.

"Yes, ma'am?"

"Are you a medical doctor or a doctor of divinity?"

"I'm a medical doctor, ma'am, and a Bachelor of Theology. A medical missionary."

"Oh. I see. Thanks very much for your trouble." She closed the door and smiled at her guests. "We seem to be staffed for any emergency. Of course his wife is working the other side of the train—a dowdy registered nurse who distributes tracts and cathartic pills."

A silence hung in the air.

"Don't you approve of medical missionaries?" Foreman asked quietly.

"Since you put it to me that bluntly, I'll be equally blunt. No. They gobbled up Hawaii, giving in return their tracts, cathartic pills and syphilis. The Nizam of Hyderabad told me last year in Karachi that the Pakistanis regard American medical missionaries as worse than Reds. It's the fashion to laugh at the Nizam as a miser, but he's a shrewd little fellow who knows a good deal more about how the natives feel and think than I do—or you do."

Foreman felt forlornly that it was a colossal bluff—but how to call it? He was one down again. And Boyce was expressing awe at her visit to India—"Not India, my dear man: Pakistan. There are zealots who'll cut your throat over that little point."—and wanting to know what it was really like—"Not as bad as most of us think here; it's a food-surplus area, you know, and in Asia that means it's a heaven on earth"—and what about the fabulous riches of the native princes—"Seventy-five percent talk, Mr. Boyce, and the rest is gold bars and precious stones stuck in the ground somewhere. The American rich live better and have more security"—and had she seen Nehru—"No; wrong country again, Mr. Boyce" and lots more. Through it all Joan Lundberg listened with awe, a little drunk besides.

It all sounded remarkably to Foreman like rehashed material from the Asia-conscious Saturday Review he read each week. He mixed himself another martini while the grand tour went on and on.

"That's enough," Mona said at last. "I'm starving. We can eat in here, you know, instead of having to buck that chow-line back there."

Then why didn't you at lunch? Foreman silently asked. Were you afraid you wouldn't make a pickup? But he rang for the porter when she asked him to.

The table was set up with Mona and Joan sitting side by side, Joan at the window seat.

During dinner the only incident of note was that the train slowed several times to a crawl, which made the lady novelist curse picturesquely.

Over coffee their hostess announced: "We're going to preserve the amenities here, even if it's got to be in a slightly bassackwards fashion. There's no drawing room for the ladies to retire to, so you men will beat it out of here for your cigars and port in the club car. After a reasonable interval one of you will say: 'Shall we join the ladies?' and then you come on back where Joan and I will have been talking women-talk. Mr. Foreman, I'll trust you to see that the port goes around the table left-handed."

On their way back to the club car Boyce asked shyly what Miss Greer had been talking about. "She's over my head sometimes, Foreman. I couldn't make out that crack about the port."

"Just a joke, I guess," Foreman said. Just a joke to make him and Boyce look like ignorant yahoos compared to suave, all-knowing Mona Greer and her intimate friend Joan Lundberg.

CHAPTER XIII

SNOW

As winter dusk closed down on the Rockies, drifting began. There's a projecting rock that has a calm lee side where the wind doesn't whisk away snow as soon as it falls. A handful of dry powdery snow accumulates there, then a bushelful that makes its own calm lee side where still more of the dry, powdery stuff can drift in.

It happens fast. The dunes grow along rocks, ridges, railroad embankments, like living things.

The first hour, six inches. The second hour, a foot. The third hour, a yard. The fourth hour, two, four or five yards until gravity won't let them grow any taller. But already they are tall enough to smother a tall man trying to flounder his way through them.

And when the sun goes down, cold clamps the Rockies like an iron vice.

CHAPTER XIV

CLUB CAR

The torpedo-shaped club car was almost filled. There were coach passengers who had no business there, nursing bottles of beer, there were the settled drinkers who had picked big chairs in early afternoon and soaked steadily from then on, nourishing themselves on sandwiches from the bar, and there were the after-dinner customers like them, rather crowded in small chairs at small tables. Just two adjacent chairs were left, and Boyce and Foreman fell into them.

"Hello there," somebody leaned over. It was Dr. Groves, of whom Mona Greer disapproved. He had a bottle of Danish beer before him, and beside him a dark little woman with snapping eyes was drinking a coke.

"Hello, doctor," Foreman said. "Did you get any business out of that sudden stop?"

"Broken right metatarsal arch in car 17," the doctor-missionary said happily. "A woman's vanity case fell on her foot from the baggage rack. My wife—this is Mrs. Groves, gentlemen, an R.N. and a lay preacher of considerable power—my wife diagnosed it and I set it."

Foreman tried futilely to rise from the little table at the introduction, but didn't make it. "How do you do, Mrs. Groves. My name's Foreman and this is Mr. Boyce. Both from Chicago."

"How do you do. My sister married a man named Foreman in Boise, Idaho. Would that have been a relative of yours?"

One of those genealogical discussions was well-launched when a neat officer's blouse trimmed with silver bars and a few campaign ribbons leaned drunkenly over the table.

"Listen, you," the first lieutenant said to Foreman. "Don't get me wrong. I'm not mad; I'm just curious. What was she driving at?"

"Who, lieutenant?" Foreman asked innocently, though he knew perfectly well.

"That lady at your table. When she called me that. What kind of a stunt was that for her to pull? What was I supposed to do, let those G.I.'s holler and bitch all they wanted to? Matterfact I lettem off easy, di'n't I?"

Well, looking at it that way, the lieutenant was right and Foreman felt a little ashamed of himself, though not much. "I don't know her well," he hedged. "She's a peculiar person. A novelist."

"Oh," the lieutenant said gravely as though that explained everything. "I see." He straightened and took the arm of a patiently-waiting slim girl with red hair. Foreman noticed that the doctor gave her a sharp, sudden glance for no good reason.

"Novelist, did you say?" Dr. Groves asked absently. "Who is, if you don't mind my asking?"

"The lady who met you at the door. She's Mona Greer. She wrote Thighs of the Wild Mare. It made a big splash in the spring."

"Oh," said the doctor unhappily. "I know. I'm afraid she's a bad one, Foreman. I use the term technically."

"She thinks you're a pretty bad one too, doctor. She has no use for medical missionaries."

"Something to drink, gentlemen?" asked the club car attendant.

"Brandy and soda for me," Foreman said. "Boyce?"

"Same, please."

They arrived in the little train bottles decreed by some mysterious working of the law of the land.

"Miss Greer," he told the medical missionary, "says the Nizam of Hyderabad told her that his people hate you people worse than they do the Reds."

"How odd," Dr. Groves said, not taking it at all personally. "I worked in Assam, in Bengal you know, and we never ran into anything like that. Of course the political and religious situations are entirely different. Hyderabad's Muslim and rather quietist, where Assam is Hindu and terribly excitable and turbulent. I never heard anything like Miss Greer's complaint against us—or the Nizam's alleged complaint."

His little wife crackled: "Come off it B.G., and say what you think. She's a blooming liar. She's a professional do-badder so naturally she hates us professional do-gooders and lies about us."

"Really, dear," Dr. Groves said deprecatingly. "I haven't any right—"

"If she's got the right to sugar-coat her poison and feed it to the public in the form of an arty novel, you've got the right to tell them what she's up to."

"Look," Foreman said hastily. "What's her book about, anyway? We've been thrown together on the train and I haven't read it. It's embarrassing."

"You're better off not to have read it," the doctor said shortly. "I did, in line of duty. (I know people laugh when you say things like that, but it's the truth.) It's a dreamy, voluptuous novel which describes the progress of a Lesbian from initiation to the point where she is initiating young girls herself. There's a great deal of hifalutin' talk in it about freedom and the right to choose one's innocent pleasures. There's not a word in it about the dreadful immorality of an older, stronger person seducing a younger, weaker person into a way of life. By extension Miss Greer's book would justify rape, bank-robbery and murder. As my wife said, it's sugar-coated poison. But I'm sorry to say that the country's book critics mostly ignored the poison and praised the sugar. The parson has said his piece, thank you."

"Good for you, B.G.," his wife said. "Finish your beer and let's have a look at that metatarsal. Glad to have met you, gentlemen. Please don't get up—you can't anyway."

After they had gone, Boyce grinned. "They surely are off the beam on Miss Greer, aren't they?" he asked.

"No, they aren't," Foreman said. "My guess is that Mona's masterpiece is straight autobiography. I think she's on the make for Miss Lundberg, for instance."

"I don't believe it!"

Foreman shrugged. "I'm not going to kill her to stop it from happening." I'm in enough trouble now.

The hayseed G.I. and a buddy were standing belligerently in the door of the club car. They spotted the chairs vacated by the doctor and his wife and took them. Shy and self-conscious, they nudged each other and muttered back and forth in a conversation that exploded occasionally into a guffaw. One of them said at last, clearly and with fake wonder: "You'd think one a these civilians ud at least buy a fightin' man a drink, wunt ya, George?"

"I sure would, Harold," the other said clearly. "I don't know whut's the matter with 'em all less'n they all tarred out from defense work."

Foreman turned and looked at them. Infantry's blue piping on their caps, but no combat badges. The piping was phony or something they thought they had a claim to after thirteen weeks of "infantry" basic training somewhere. On their lapels were the flaming-bomb insignia of the Ordnance Corps. ETO ribbon with stars. Good conduct ribbon. Occupation ribbon. The corporal had a Bronze Star ribbon and the p.f.c. did not.

"Let's get out of here," he said to Boyce, who followed him. Swaying down the aisles of the successive cars, he thought, What the hell do they leave a person? Can a man live without pride? Does he have the right to?

There was another one of the sudden stops. The speed of the train was less this time but the brakes had been thrown on more violently. They both went sprawling in the aisle between green-curtained pullman berths from which came men's sulphurous curses and women's nervous cries. A child was shrieking hysterically somewhere.

"You all right?" Foreman gasped, picking himself up. He gave Boyce his hand and tugged the slighter man to his feet.

"Nothing broken," Boyce said. Heads popped out from the green curtains as they proceeded cautiously. "Foreman, I don't believe it. I can't believe it."

"Maybe because if you believed it you'd have to do something about it. And you know you aren't very good at doing things."

"Look," the rug man blustered. "Who do you think you are that you have the right to talk like that to me? You aren't an old friend or a preacher or a psychoanalyst, so just lay off that stuff."

"She's your girl, not mine."

The little man stopped in the aisle and absurdly took him by the lapel. "Just what the hell do you mean by that, Foreman?"

"Take your hand off me. I meant exactly what I said. You're riding with her, you know her a couple of hours longer than I do and what're you getting so hot about?"

"I'm sorry," Boyce muttered. "I'm on edge." They trudged on, balancing themselves nervously against the moment when the train would start again. It did, smoothly, and slowly.

"What's that?" Foreman asked.

"I said," Boyce told him, "that I wish she was my girl. Me a married man. Isn't that a laugh? But she's a nice kid. Long-winded about politics but I figure she'll drop that when she gets what she needs."

"Now who's being a psychoanalyst?" Foreman grinned.

As they passed a roomette door it swung open. A fat, pale-faced, sweating girl in a tent-like nightgown said hoarsely, clinging to the doorframe: "Please. A doctor. I think my pains are coming on."

"Pains," said Foreman, studying her blankly. "Pains! Oh God!" He put his arm around her and let her weight sag on him. "Help me get her into the berth, Boyce. Easy …"

"We won't be a minute, kid," he told the fat girl. "There's a fine doctor on the train and his wife's a registered nurse. We'll hunt him up right away and be right back. Boyce, you go back and I'll go forward. Don't be shy. Yell your head off."

He started forward, bawling: "Doctor Groves! Mrs. Groves!" without stopping. Three cars up their heads popped out of a roomette. "Lady's going to have a baby, doctor," he said.

"Let's go," the doctor-preacher said. "Bring my kit, Nan."

"Right with you, B.G."

When they got back to the labor room two women with their hair in curlers were holding the fat girl's hands and telling her horror stories about their own confinements. She was laughing at them.

"Hysterical, doctor," one of them told Groves in a voice of doom.

"Out," the doctor gestured briskly to all of them. "Mr. Foreman, will you please try to find the conductor and send him here."

Foreman collected Boyce and the conductor together. The conductor was telling Boyce that he'd put him off the train if he didn't stop yelling and go to bed. It was quickly straightened out.

"Conductor," the newsman asked, "where can we put her off?"

"Don't worry about it, mister," the conductor said testily, toddling ahead of him and making better speed with his old legs that were used to the jolting roadbed than either of the younger men.

"What did he say?" asked Boyce, catching up.

"He said nothing. I think maybe we're on the big upgrade now. Next stop, the coastal valley of California."

"He could radio for an ambulance to meet us... even a helicopter!"

"Helicopter's out. Maybe ambulance is too. Maybe everything's out except a man on snowshoes. There's a lot of snow out there. I'm scared for that butterball in the roomette."

They rapped on the door of Mona's compartment. Joan opened the door, her head half-turned in a laughing comment to her hostess.

"You dawdled over your cigars, gentlemen." Mona smiled like a cat. "While you were dawdling there's been a slight rearrangement ..."

"It was a medical emergency," Foreman said.

"Lady's having a baby three cars down," Boyce added. "We got the doctor for her."

Joan looked stunned. "A...a fat girl? Quite young?"

"That's right."

"I know this is silly. But did she happen to mention the Galapagos Islands?"

Mona laughed indulgently and Foreman said, stunned: "No. Should she have?"

"I thought she might have. I talked with her this afternoon. She's from the Galapagos Islands. She thinks she's ..." Joan sat down, her face white.

It was going to be so cozy, she thought vaguely. I was going to move in with Mona tonight and come what may. And now this absurd girl is having her baby and I don't want to move in with Mona... not now. Because the girl reminded me that I'm a woman? Because the thought of her would be a skeleton at the feast? Because compared to her the brilliant Mona Greer looks somehow... dirty?

It was all vague, formless and took less than a second.

"What's the matter, little one?" Mona was demanding. "Another drop of brandy?" She poured but Joan waved it away.

"No, thanks. Not brandy, or anything at all. This girl seemed quite sure that she was going to die in childbirth. It upset me. Mona, thanks for your kind offer but I think I'll stay in my upper berth tonight. It's silly, but I'd rather be alone after hearing about her."

"Very well, little one. Perhaps tomorrow night."

"Thank you very much, Mona. I'm truly grateful. Perhaps tomorrow night." She went distractedly from the compartment.

Mona Greer yawned daintily and glanced at her traveling clock.

"My," said Foreman like an automaton. "I-did-not-realize-the-lateness-of-the-hour. Goodnight-and-thank-you-for-a-lovely-evening-Miss-Greer."

Her eyes shot loathing at them as they closed the door.

Standing in the corridor Boyce shrugged helplessly. "What can I do against somebody like that?" he mumbled, dropping his eyes. "What chance have I got?"

"Don't ask me for advice," Foreman exploded. "She's your girl. I have troubles of my own." He stalked off to his own roomette knowing that Boyce was following him with a helpless, pleading look.

CHAPTER XV

SNOW

Daniel Menafee squinted into the bright tunnel that the train's glaring headlight bored through the wall of snow.

"Trouble," he mumbled.

Nothing felt right under his hands. The giant power plant was roaring and straining, and the train should have been thundering along at sixty-five miles per hour to make up schedule. Instead it groaned ahead, shoving, shoving, shoving through drifts that hid the rails.

The blunt prow of the diesel locomotive battered at a new mountain of snow that loomed into the glaring headlight. The dial showed a crazy seventy miles per hour, but that was only the revolutions of the drive wheels, grinding futilely against the rails.

The train had stopped.

CHAPTER XVI

GREEN CURTAINS

Boyce lay in the swaying darkness of his lower berth hearing the hundred night-sounds of a pullman car. His watch said 1:05.

Coughs, belches, creaking mattresses, the slam of a distant door somewhere, the clickety-clack of the rails, the shivering effort of the giant diesel-electrics thrumming through the whole length of the train. The clickety-clack slowed and slowed and stopped at last. But it didn't matter. In all but body, Boyce was in the berth above. He grinned bitterly and secretly as he heard Joan in the berth above twist about on the mattress. She was having no better a night than he, but he had to pretend that the green curtain was an invincible barrier, like six inches of hardened steel. He couldn't say to her: "You're worried and I'm lonesome. Let's be friends."

At 1:17 he heard her struggle into dressing gown and slippers. She didn't ring for the porter and his ladder. Her slippered toe groped for a moment inches from his nose and found the edge of his berth and he heard her other foot hit the floor of the aisle. Her toe vanished as suddenly as it had appeared.

Boyce didn't hear her walk off down the aisle. He drew his green curtain aside and said: "Joan?"

She jumped. "Oh. Did I wake you? I'm sorry." She was pretending. She knew he hadn't been able to sleep, just as surely as he had known about her.

"No," he said. "I couldn't sleep. Will you talk to me?"

"Certainly not here," she whispered.

"Vacant berth up there they didn't make up."

"All right," she said, and glided off into the dim-lit car.

Boyce struggled into his own robe and...a traveling man's reflex... slipped his wallet into its pocket.

She was waiting, her feet primly together and her hands in her lap, looking through the window at blackness.

"Hello," he said, sitting beside her.

"I hope that girl's all right," she said. "I wonder where we are. We don't seem to be moving."

"We've been on the road about 16 hours. Raton Pass, I suppose. Then down we go to the coastal plain."

"I hope that girl's all right. She's an awfully strange person. Imagine meeting somebody from the Galapagos Islands ..." Her voice was becoming brittle with hysteria and the words she spoke seemed to be separate things, not parts of sentences that told you what she thought and felt. "... of all places. She made me feel ignorant. I went to college, but she knew things I'd never heard of. South American history, music, medicine. She thinks she's going to die. And I don't think she minds. What do you think of Mona?"

Boyce said: "She's smart. And lovely. And heartless."

"No-she-isn't. She was perfectly wonderful to me. She's warm and friendly. Sheltering ..."

The girl was trembling beside him. "I wonder if she's awake too," she said. "I might stop by and see. She was very good to me, offering to share her compartment. Don't you think so?"

Boyce performed the first act of heroism of his life. He broke clean through the mould that had been cast around him at birth and had been hardening ever since.

"No, I don't think so," he said. "I think she's a wolf. I think she's going to talk you into things you don't want to do and then break your heart for kicks." His own heart was thumping wildly. "Don't let her, darling ..."

"You shouldn't talk like that," she said mechanically, dreamily. "You're married ..."

"Yes," he said dully. "I'm married. I'm forty years old. Old enough to know better. I wish... never mind."

"What do you wish?" she asked.

"I daydream sometimes," he said. His voice was almost inaudible. He was glad she couldn't see his face. "About having kids. And a house where I can put my feet on the furniture if I want to. And having a job that makes me sweat and gives me an appetite and lets me sleep at night. And a wife who... liked me. My wife doesn't like me, Joan. She doesn't like children. Or feet on the furniture. Or small towns. Or men who sweat for a living."

"It's too late now," Joan said flatly. "You married her."

"Yes," Boyce said. "I married her. Or she married me. I guess she married me. You saw from her picture that she's no raving beauty. I guess she decided I was as good as she could do. I'm a shrimp but I'm a hard worker. So she wore tight sweaters and she rubbed up against me when we danced and she let me paw her. Then one night in Grant Park... she wasn't a virgin but I was too dumb to know that because she said it hurt. Then she said she was pregnant. Only she wasn't." His voice had sunk to a haunted whisper.

Nice little guy, Joan thought sadly. Hooked for good. Even if he was a man, even if men pushed you around and...

The image of her father intruded, and with it the cloud of rage that it aroused in her.

"My father was a monster," she said slowly and poisonously. "He was a brainy, brilliant, sparkling, attractive monster. I think he must have had a woman a week. He killed my mother with his brains and brilliance. He made my life a hell on earth to the day he died. And after. You've no business feeling smug because you're a downtrodden male. Women get kicked in the teeth too. By men."

"Don't you want children? You another one of those people that think they don't matter?"

Joan began to cry. Yes; she wanted children.

He put his arm tentatively around her and felt first her stiffening and shrinking, and then slow relaxation against his arm. "I'm afraid," she said, flatly. There were no more tears.

"Of being hurt?"

"Of that. And of tying myself to a man. I know what they can do to you. What they... he... did to my mother." But her shoulders were relaxed against his arm. She's reminding herself of how she thinks she ought to be, Boyce thought cloudily.

The porter appeared in his white, round-collared coat and took in the picture of them and thought he understood. In his softest, most impersonal after-dark voice he said delicately: "Folks, there's a no-show drawingroom in the next cyah seems a pity to waste if you cain't sleep. An' the pullman conductor he won't know if you set there a while. I don' wake him up until four-thirty o'clock."

Joan went stiff against his arm... but didn't speak. Boyce said: "That's very kind of you," to the porter. He took his arm from around the girl's shoulders and gave the porter a five-dollar bill from his wallet.

"Thank you suh!" he beamed. "Step this way, folks."

"Joan," Boyce said. She rose like a sleepwalker and followed the porter.

The sudden cold in the vestibule between the cars was startling. It bit through his pyjamas and robe and then was gone as they emerged into the dimness of the next car. The porter opened a door and said: "Heah 'tis, folks. I see you have a watch, suh." Delicate reminder.

"Yes. Thanks." He closed the door on him. Joan was standing by the window.

"Afraid?" he said.

"Yes. Terribly. Where's this going to end? It can't just stop here. The thing is... with Mona, it could."

"That's right. With her it wouldn't be love. It would be an imitation of love."

"That word," she said. "Do you love me? Do I love you? I don't know. But I like being in here with you. I want to do things for you. I want you to like me. If anybody hurts you I want to claw their eyes out. Is that being in love?"

"That's about all there is to it," he said.

She laughed shakily. "Turn out the light," she said. She was scared clear through to the marrow of her bones and she didn't want him to know. He was a nice little guy…

He found her in the dark and took her hand. It balled into a fist when he touched it, with a rigidity that made her a woman of stone. "Oh," the rug man said in a low, sick voice, "what that bastard did to you."

"I'm sorry. I can't help it. Truly, I can't," she whispered.

"Sit here with me." She did, and leaned timidly against him. He kissed her. Her lips were like marble.

She stood up and said in a dull monotone: "It's no use. I'm no good for you. I wish I were, but I'm not. That's all there is to it. I'm sorry I'm such a fool and I'm sorry this hurts you, but I can't do anything about it …"

She blundered from the drawing room.

Boyce sat in the dark, still with pain. It's too late now, he thought. You weren't man enough to make her want you. You've missed the last bus. Nobody else like that is going to come along. Very soon you'll be forty, soon you'll be fifty, soon you'll be sixty and soon you'll be dead without ever having known love.

And her? Perhaps for her the imitation of love in the Mona-monster's arms, the imitation that carried no responsibilities except not to get caught by the cops.

He got up tiredly and walked back through the hundred night-noises… snores, coughs, creaks, stirrings… to his own berth and went to bed.

Above him, in her own green-curtained privacy, he again heard Joan stirring restlessly, like a story-book princess locked up in the cold tower of her own body.

CHAPTER XVII

SNOW

The B-25 bucked and heaved in dawn convection currents over the Rockies.

The pilot wrenched the wheel hard over, fighting for trim in the choppy air. "You see anything?" he asked the copilot.

"Snow," the copilot said, profoundly.

"Ho-ho, that's rich," the pilot said. "Are we over Raton Pass?"

"Don't know. Never did learn to navigate."

"Don't think I think you're kidding. Look for that goddam train, will you?"

"Why?"

"That's a very good question, my friend. I wish I knew the answer. Operation Horseturd they ought to call this one."

"There it is, I guess," the copilot said, pointing. It was a black thread on a rumpled white sheet far below.

"Good for you. Take a couple of pictures and hook up the static line to the chutes."

When the pictures were snapped and the static line hooked the pilot opened his bomb bay. Five bunches of medical supplies and food tumbled out and blossomed parachutes.

"Gonna land about twenty miles north of the train," the copilot said.

"Tough tittie," the pilot said. "What am I supposed to do about it… land, climb out and hand them to the conductor? We'll be lucky sons of bitches if we get home in one piece the way it is."

"It looks," brooded the copilot, "as if that train is going to stay right there for a good long while."

"Operation Horseturd," mumbled the pilot as they headed for home.

* * * *

Far below a wolf whimpered and shrank against a rock. There was no scent of game, hot-blooded game or offal for him to tear. There was only cold and snow and hunger racking his gaunt frame.

* * * *

In their own corner of the train, unguessed-at by passengers, the porters were talking.

"How'd you make out, boy?"

"Couple of hams over. Kinda short on blankets."

"Gimme a ham for two blankets."

A third, for the love of mischief, pretended to be shocked. "A whole ham for two bitty blankets?" he exclaimed. "Man, don't you deal with him."

The porter with the blankets turned a baleful eye on the trouble-maker. "Advise you to keep out of this deal, Hoops."

"Who's gonna make me, man?"

"I got a good old friend on the Spirit of California getting a little tired of that run. You like this run here, don't you, Hoops? Got a gal in Frisco you visit with. My friend has you beat on seniority by eighteen months and he'd just as soon bump you off this train as not—for a friend. You like to get bumped down to that L.A. run and stop seeing your Frisco gal, Hoops? Well, what you say, Hoops?"

"I say nothing, Mister Cutshaw," grinned Hoops. "My lips are sealed, Mr. Cutshaw, sir."

"They better be," said Cutshaw. "How about it?" he asked the porter with the hams.

"You got a deal, Cutshaw."

Hoops chattered: "Anybody wants to make a good deal, he can if he got some H or maybe C."

Cutshaw glared at him. "You buying? By God, Hoops, I'll turn you in if I catch you with white stuff on the train!" He picked up Hoops by his collarless white jacket and shook him. "Brother Hoops, where you got it?"

Hoops yelled: "Put me down, you crazy fool! I don't mean for me. I mean that red-headed gal, the second-john's wife in sixty-three! I was just kidding that she's gonna be bustin' for a fix if she runs out while we're stalled."

Cutshaw let go. "Very sorry," he said. "I'll give you half a ham first chance I get. I lost my temper—you know how I feel about it."

"Well, Cutshaw, I didn't mean to call you crazy and thanks for the half a ham. And you don't need to worry about me flirting with Rule Sixty-One. Hoops is a man that likes his job." Rule Sixty-One is the prohibition law of the American railroads—instant dismissal for any employee under the influence of liquor or narcotics while on the job.

* * * *

The red-headed woman, Mrs. Richard Claiborn Moody III, was not asleep. Her husband, in the upper berth of their compartment, stirred quietly and then asked: "Joyce?"

"We haven't started yet," she said.

"We'll be going by morning," he said. "They have snow plows, things. I won't miss the boat."

"It's a plane," she said.

"Figure of speech," he yawned. "Figures of speech are always a little behind the times. Joyce, is anything wrong?" From up there he could feel her tenseness.

"I think I'll have a nightcap," she said.

"Pthuh! I couldn't take a drink now if you paid me. But I've been asleep. Haven't you?"

"No." She got out of the berth and poured a large Scotch in a tumbler. She drank it down and went back to bed. Still tense.

"What gets me," her husband rambled, "is being under Navy control. The Air Force you can reason with. At least they have the same vehicular specifications. Well, it's only a year and I need it for the record. Then, by God, my captaincy and a company. I hope it's some place civilized so you can live on the post."

"And have your platoon leaders' wives buttering up me for a change."

"Well, that's the way it goes. You were swell with Mrs. Hertz, by the way—did I tell you?"

"Old cow."

"Yes dear, but a colonel's old cow. You were swell, though."

As the conversation drifted quite another part of Joyce Moody's mind was very busy with arithmetic. Over and over she was computing that one and one and one and one are four and no more, and that she had counted on the four to take her to the Coast, where she knew of a clerk in a hotel pharmacy. She had used three, and there was one left, in her handbag. Perhaps the three had been cut more heavily than usual, because the yen was on her too early. Liquor didn't help, liquor never helped though she always tried it.

She was quietly angry with her husband and the United States Army; between them they had seen to it that she became defiled and an addict. The long hours of his unpredictable tour of duty, the night shifts at the Pentagon, the weekend tricks he had pulled—what on earth could anybody expect except what had happened? Naturally old Charlie had shown up, kind and attentive. Naturally Rickey had been pleased that this pleasant man of forty-five who had known Joyce as a child was escorting her here and there while he was on duty. Naturally they had wound up in bed together while Rickey was working through an unbroken forty-eight hours during the Quemoy flap. Naturally old Charlie had offered her the harmless white powder and naturally she had tried it.

And got hooked.

She opened her handbag and by feel found the little packet. She spread half the powder on her thumbnail and sniffed it sharply into her left nostril and then the rest into her right.

"Catching cold, dear?" Rickey asked from above, concerned.

"No," she said. The good feeling was beginning to spread, and she was almost able to forget that now there were none left at all.

"Hope I get a good G-S," said Rickey. "Funny, but those civilians can make you or break you. Biffy Welch over at Chateauroux has a marvelous boy, G-S 12, used to be an Ordnance sergeant, runs his vehicle section like clockwork. Dear?"

"Yes?"

"Remember what I told you? About if the balloon goes up?"

"I remember."

"Well—remember it. Think I'll sleep now."

"Good night." And then she could sleep too, though there were none left at all.

* * * *

Foreman looked about his roomette and then at his traveling clock. It was an early-morning hour and the train was not moving. He said aloud: "You stupid bastard, what have you got yourself into?"

He had begun to suspect that he would never sleep again. He unpacked his gladstone far enough to find a bottle of Scotch picked up at the station liquor shop on an impulse. "Jolly old impulse, what?" he said, and wrestled with the seal. The bottle opened and he paused to consider what came next. Did you ring the porter for a shot glass? God, no. Ridiculous. You poured it into a tumbler and drank from the tumbler, like a hotel-room drunk. He poured a big one and swallowed it.

"I suppose," he said, "I ought to jot this down. Date and time. Foreman's First Solitary Drink."

It was that. He had reached his thirties without taking a drink by himself in private. Getting mildly drunk at a bar did not count; neither did cocktails before lunch or dinner. Opening a bottle all by himself, expecting nobody to join him, and taking a drink was something he had never done before. It had never occurred to him that it might be a pleasant or profitable thing to do, so he had never done it.

It tasted like any other jolt of straight medium-priced Scotch, and his vague expectation that it would immediately relax him and send him stumbling sleepily in the direction of his berth was not fulfilled. He had another, sitting up, and that did nothing either.

Maybe this is how they do it, he reflected. He thought of Mike Sullivan, and shuddered. Mike had been one of his buck-an-hour desk men for a month. A jewel, a treasure for the first week, until payday. Fast, accurate, intelligent, untemperamental except for a very faint flavor of contempt for the unethical side of the operation. He wasn't a child who could be kidded into thinking it was routine to steal the news. He was an experienced news-man and it was wonderful, until payday.

Mike was supposed to come back after dinner and take over until closing at 11 P.M. Mike showed up at 9:30 P.M. with peppermint on his breath, unable to hit the teletype keys. He sent him home after getting him to understand that he could damn well pull the Saturday shift instead. Saturday morning, no Mike. He phoned him at home and Mike's mother, very Ould Sod, said the boy's stomach was a weechy bit upset and could Misther Foreman plase excuse him for the day. Mr. Foreman excused him and worked the Saturday and Sunday tricks, and Mike came in on Monday with apologies and was wonderful again for a week—until payday. That weekend he did not get over until Tuesday, and Foreman had a little talk with him, the upshot of which was that Mike's paycheck would be mailed to his mother. It's the best thing, said Mike; I can't control it. If I still had my faith I could take the pledge, but I've lost my faith. Mike was fine until Friday. It had not occurred to Foreman that when Mike got home and his mother gave him the check to endorse, the inevitable would happen. It hap-pened, and there was no Mike McGowan until Tuesday again. He came in very sick, unable to work. Foreman sent him home to rest up and he came in on Wednesday and was fine until payday. That time the check had been made out, by special dispensation from New York, to Mike's mother. On payday Mike jimmied open the petty cash box when he was alone on the night shift, typed an apologetic note and went out to get fried. He showed up Monday, drunk and weeping and promising to make restitution of the thirty-five dollars. Foreman told him to forget about the money and to come back if he ever got straightened out; meanwhile there was no job for him there. Evidently Mike never did get straightened out. Somehow later he got to believing that the service owed him thirty-five dollars, and would phone late at night from bars to demand his rights. All new deskmen had to be alerted to those calls from Mike; if you weren't prepared for them they were an eerie experience. What he was living and drinking on, God alone knew. Perhaps his mother.

Poor Mike, thought Foreman, and looked at the Scotch bottle.

It was half empty.

Foreman got to his feet and noticed that he was quite drunk. "Did I do that?" he asked fuzzily, staring at the bottle. "Must have."

He fell onto the bed in a heavy, dreamless sleep.

* * * *

The old lady in Drawing Room C said to her husband: "Harvey, wake up!"

He woke from the thin and precious sleep of extreme old age. "What is it? What happened?"

"I've decided," she said. "I'll plant the border with pompom zinnias, then behind them foxgloves, and behind them delphiniums—Guineveres."

"Splendid," he said, and rolled over. They did not know yet that they would never see their garden bloom again.

CHAPTER XVIII

THE CORRUPTED

Foreman woke at seven-thirty in the stalled train with a bad headache, sour stomach and all the other classic symptoms of a hangover. Aspirin didn't help. Sitting woozily on the edge of his berth he contemplated his bottle and unscrewed the cap. The smell made him retch, but he choked down a mouthful of whisky.

Hollywood would love me for this, he thought sourly. The cliché of the newspaperman-drunk. The liquor began to take hold after an alarming moment when he thought he was going to lose it. He lit a cigarette and found his electric shaver. If there was an outlet in his compartment, he couldn't find it. Foreman got into his shirt and pants and stumped down the swaying aisle to the men's room.

The morning rush was on. The three outlets labeled "110-volt DC" were occupied, and he got a hostile glare or two from men carrying electric razors of their own and waiting their turn. Everybody was bitching about the unscheduled stop. The unwashed smell was bad, and one fat character in an undershirt who could have used a brassiere was carefully perforating a pre-breakfast cigar with a wooden match. With concentration he put it in his mouth and drew experimentally. All was well. He struck the wooden match, let the sulfur burn out and lit the cigar, sucking wetly on it, turning it in his mouth to the tip of flame, puffing grey clouds of smoke.

Foreman's stomach churned in him and he fled from the room, caroming into Dr. Groves. The medical missionary was looking healthy and handsome in a fresh white shirt. "Good morning, Mr. Foreman," he said cheerfully.

"Morning, doctor. Excuse the body-block. I thought I was going to throw up in there. Oh, that cigar-smoke."

"Medically speaking, you'll feel better if you do throw up." The doctor's clear eyes were assessing his red-rimmed ones and undoubtedly he smelled the sour stomach of last night's drinking and the reek of the morning bracer on his breath. "I can give you some tartar emetic."

"Ooh." Foreman passed his hand across his greasy, clammy brow. "Maybe you'd better, doctor. Oh, that cigar …"

"Be right back." The doctor disappeared and Foreman counted the contractions of his stomach until he came back. After eleven flip-flops the doctor was handing him a quarter of a five-grain tablet. "Dissolve it in a little water and drink it. It's very fast and thorough."

"Thanks a lot. How's the girl?"

"A false alarm. Her contractions tapered off into nothing. But it's going to be soon. I wish we could have her taken off the train."

Automatically, they both glanced at the white-shrouded country outside, like a ghost-land. You could see conical white humps that were drifted-in pine trees. The doctor shrugged and went into the men's room.

Foreman drew a paper cup of water and took it into his compartment. The emetic fizzed for a moment as he dropped it in. It was the bitterest stuff he had ever tasted—a kind of super-quinine. The doctor was right. It was very fast. He barely had time to raise the lid of the dinky little toilet before it hit. And the doctor was right again. It was very thorough. After three very long minutes Foreman flopped onto his cot feeling much weaker and much better. He mopped his brow and decided that life was worth living.

There was a feel of immense effort trembling through the fabric of the train. Its twin-unit diesel electric locomotive, a city block long and crammed with power, should be whipping the immensely heavy train along at an average fifty miles per hour. But it was stopped dead.

These were the mountains, and they were tough babies. Not so long ago, in the early Victorian era when ladies and gentlemen in Europe were dancing the schottische and the new-fangled waltz, not far from here at right about this time of year the Donner party was stranded by snow. Before it was spring, men had killed and eaten other men to survive.

And snow made you think of other things: serving an 81-millimeter mortar in Hürtgen Forest, the lovely, balsam-scented natural tank-trap planted on the German frontier. All the pine trees were Christmas trees, trimmed with strips of tinsel…anti-radar "window" dropped by bombers on their way to the Ruhr or Berlin. Any of the pine trees might be a man-trap, crashing onto you and crushing you at a puff of wind that took it the right way. Hürtgen Forest had been fought over three times, and shell fragments riddled and weakened the trees almost invisibly. And, as in all forests, you had to be very, very careful about a clear field of fire for your mortar. Crews were wiped out when the ascending shell hit a stray branch on the way up and exploded.

And death made you think of other things: the man with crabs eating his face that might be you if you failed in Frisco or if you talked out of turn to the red-faced, prosy, short-of-breath businessmen whose business was gambling, pimping, dope-running and, whenever necessary, murder.

Why had he not feared death in the Hürtgen Forest, but feared it now, so bitterly that he was abjectly taking orders from men who were not different in any essential way from the Nazis he had fought?

He tried not to answer the question, but the answer came: because you're corrupted now by a few years of lying to yourself every minute of the day; because you took their money and pretended it wasn't theirs; because you pretended you were Larry Foreman of World Wireless instead of Larry Foreman the Syndicate Stooge. Now you know? Like hell. You knew it all along. The shrimp cocktails, the steaks, the good suits, the pretty girls, the good apartment... they were paid for with the housewife's dollar bet at the horse-room, the patched-pants Negro porter's nickel hopefully invested in a policy number that will never come up, the high-school junkie's stolen five-dollar bill for a cap of well-cut heroin, the out-of-town buyer's fifty dollars for an infected call girl who will be methodically beaten up if she tries to quit the life.

And what comes next? None of your goddamned business, fella. You're not paid to think. You're paid to go to Frisco and set up a chain of what the newspapers will call "nerve centers of gambling" quickly, economically and efficiently. You're paid to set up a smooth-running machine to siphon money from the pockets of San Francisco residents and visitors into the pockets of the prosy, short-of-breath businessmen who will do with it God knows what. Buy yachts? Real estate? Diamonds and furs for their wives and women?

He didn't want to think about it. He didn't want to think about it.

"Hollywood, I salute you," he said slowly, and took a long, burning drink from the Scotch bottle.

So he had problems. Who didn't? Boyce and the blonde had problems. La Greer had problems... or would in a few years.

A discreet tap on the door. "Make up your berth, suh?"

"Okay," he called. Might as well try to shave again. He collected his gear and went to the washroom feeling light-headed. The liquor had hit his empty stomach hard and fast. He shaved and washed and went back to his compartment, where he had another drink and finished dressing for breakfast.

In the crowded vestibule of the diner he was jammed up against the lieutenant and his red-headed lady. Being jammed up against the lady was not disagreeable, but he disengaged himself with a mumbled apology.

"Morning," the lieutenant said. "How's the lady writer? Is it safe for me to show my face in public?"

"Matter of fact, lieutenant, I'd hide if I were you. The last time I saw her she was oiling a .38 and asking what car you were in."

The red-headed girl laughed sharply and said to her husband: "How terrible for you, darling. You're going to be shot by a celebrity in a streamliner instead of being cut down by the first invasion wave."

"Zip it up," he said to her quickly.

"Sorry, darling. Security's involved, isn't it? Darling—if the lady writer shoots you, do I get a Purple Heart anyway?"

"Nope. Non-service-connected when you get shot by a lady writer," the lieutenant said, cheerful again. "But you get the insurance. That'll be nice, won't it?"

"Yum-yum. I'll say it is. I can't wait to get my hands on that ten grand and make a clean sweep through Carson, Pirie and Scott. They'll adore you on State Street for making the supreme sacrifice, dear."

The lieutenant looked alarmed at her wild, loud talk—more so when the man in front of them turned around and looked blankly at them both. He was fat and middle-aged and mournful. "You're being very witty about Purple Hearts and insurance, young lady," he told the lieutenant's wife in a wondering voice. "I lost my boy in Korea myself, at Inchon, so I can really appreciate your humor. Excuse me." He pushed past them and through the crowd.

The lieutenant turned to his wife and said hesitantly: "That kind of talk, Joyce. I've asked you before—"

The red-head said chattily to Foreman: "We're service people so we have to watch our step, you know. Conduct detrimental to discipline and efficiency. Death or such other punishment as a court martial may inflict."

"Are you drunk?" Foreman asked, really interested.

"Look, mister," said the lieutenant to him.

"I apologize," Foreman said, meaning it. The poor guy appeared to have troubles enough. "As a matter of fact, I've had a couple of drinks myself. I'm a newspaperman and of course you've been to the movies so you know how we are."

"No," said the lieutenant. "I don't know how newspapermen are but I can smell your breath and it makes me sick."

"Lieutenant, I apologized," Foreman said gently. "Or I tried to. Maybe the apology was a little uncouth, but that's because I was only a staff sergeant."

The red-head put in helpfully: "I've been to the movies. I know how staff sergeants are."

Foreman saw suddenly that her eyes were odd: the pupils contracted to pin-points, even in the meager light of the vestibule. My God, he thought. A junkie. The poor guy. He didn't say anything, the lieutenant didn't say anything, and after her crack the red-head didn't say anything.

The little diner attendant shuffled up and said to him: "Yes, sir. Room for one. Seat you in a moment, sir. With the gentleman you had lunch with," he beamed, as if asking: won't that be nice?

Oh, God. Little Boyce and his troubles. But he'd be nice to him. He was drunker than he thought. The last thing he'd wanted was a spat with anybody.

Boyce was moodily eating scrambled eggs. "Good morning," he said to Foreman.

"Good morning." To the waiter: "I'll have the same." To Boyce: "Look, I'm sorry if I talked out of turn last night. I seem to remember being loaded."

"It's all right. Things look different in the morning, don't they? 'The cold light of dawn.' Late at night you get a couple of drinks into you and you think you can lick the world, do what you want, have everything your own way. Comes the dawn. And you realize you were acting like a jerk and nothin's going to be changed, ever."

The poor little guy. Change the subject before he starts to bawl. "That girl who was going to have the baby. She isn't. The doctor said it was a false alarm this time. But he's sweating bullets about getting her off the train."

"Into that?" Boyce gestured half-heartedly at the window, at the white-robed landscape of rocks, drifts and pine trees.

Foreman's coffee, eggs and toast arrived. He drank the coffee and played with the food. "How's Miss Lundberg?" he asked at last.

Uncontrollably, a spasm of pain went over the little man's face. In a flat, precise tone he said: "I saw her for a little while this morning. She said she thought she'd say hello to Mona and perhaps have breakfast with her."

"Something happened."

"Yes, something happened. I tried to make love to her last night. This isn't kissing-and-telling because nothing happened. Nothing happened because I did a poor damn bungling job of it. I said the wrong things and I did the wrong things and if I did any right things I didn't do them well enough...

"I don't know. Excuse me." He dropped a bill on the cardboard check and hurried off.

Foreman chewed a corner of toast slowly. Corruption knows corruption. The same seduction that the Syndicate business had practiced on him was being practiced on Joan Lundberg. They had found his weak spot and worked on it. Mona Greer had found Joan Lundberg's weak spot and was working on it overtime. He, sitting there, was by now a tool of despicable men who, like the Nazis, wanted the world with a fence around it and did not care one damn how they got it or who got hurt in the getting. Joan soon might be a tool of a despicable woman who wanted kicks and did not care one damn how she got them or who got hurt in the getting.

The attendant seated across the table from him the fat, mournful man who had told off the lieutenant's junkie wife. Apparently remembered grief had not kept him away from the pleasures of eating very long. "Morning," he said to Foreman, without recognition. He briskly checked a great many items on the menu and said to the newsman: "Great day for penguins, huh?"

"Sure is."

"What's your line, if you don't mind my asking?"

"I'm a news man."

"I'll be darned. I used to be a newspaperman myself. On the old Wichita Beacon."

Sure. Everybody used to be a newspaperman himself. Two weeks as a bookkeeper for the Pismo Beach Shopping News and for the rest of your life you used to be a newspaperman yourself, boring and annoying the man with a real title to the name.

"The hell you were," he said to the man.

The man completely ignored the remark, as though it had not been made. "Those were the days," he chuckled.

Foreman tried again. He asked nastily: "Were you on the news side or the business side, mister?"

"Business side, as a matter of fact. I was a space salesman. But my heart was always with the reporter. I was always hanging around the city room. They lead a fascinating life. Dangerous, too. Fires, accidents, highballing through the red lights if a story breaks—I wonder if you've ever thought of the advantages of special accident coverage to a newsman? I happen to be in the insurance line, here's my card, William (Bill) Loober, Professional Building, Wichita, like it says there, Mister—what did you say your name was?"

Foreman took the card and told him and the spiel flowed on. Loober was a very good salesman, he noted impersonally. He liked the man; he radiated warmth; he made you like him. He interested you.

But he should not be likeable, warm and interesting now. A wound in him had been opened and salt rubbed in it by the lady junkie's vicious joke. Bill Looper minutes after that had happened should still be smarting and morose, wishing vainly that the Red sniper had missed or the U.N. artillery shell had not been a short or that the Mig pilot had not pressed the firing button.

Who, Foreman wondered impersonally, had corrupted Bill Looper and to what end?

Who had emptied Looper of grief over a dead son and filled him with the lust to make a buck and spend it on television sets, show seats, convertibles, watches, deep freezers that would never bring back his son?

CHAPTER XIX

SNOW

The conductor and the engineer are conferring worriedly in the cabin of the diesel-electric locomotive.

Daniel Manafee, close to hysteria, says: "I don't give a Goddamn how many people you have aboard. We're snowbound and we're not going anywheres until the plows come and dig us out. And Christ knows when that's going to be."

The elderly, peppery conductor snaps: "A hell of a railroad man you turned out to be. What about later in the day? Won't the sun soften it up some? What about that?"

"My God, man, it's forty-fifty below out there. If the sun softens it up it'll just freeze rock-hard again. We're stuck, I tell you. Stuck."

"How about light and heat?"

The engineer studies his fuel-oil gauges. "Maybe a dozen of both. I ought to cut out the lighting circuits so we'll have heat longer—"

"No you don't! Turn off the lights and well have a panic aboard like you never saw."

Nothing is solved, and the conductor stumps angrily back through the block-long diesels into the passenger cars, scowling and getting ready to lie like a man.

CHAPTER XX

PRECAUTIONS

The morning rush in the ladies' room was like feeding time in a parakeet ranch. Amid the din Joan heard that the fat girl's pregnancy had not yet come to term. The pullman maid was able to tell her the car and compartment number. She dressed hurriedly and did not pause as she passed Mona Greer's door.

Joan rapped timidly on the door of the fat girl's compartment. Unexpected result: the next door down opened and a dark little woman wearing no makeup popped out to demand: "What do you want?"

"Why, I'd spoken to, uh, the patient and I thought I might pay a visit—"

"She's asleep," the little woman snapped. "I'm Mrs. Groves. I'm a nurse. The conductor was kind enough to move out her neighbor so I could keep an eye on her."

"Oh, that's splendid. How is she?"

"Her pains have stopped and she's sleeping without sedation. That's all anyone could wish for."

"I'm very glad." She saw suddenly that the little woman was dog-tired, almost out on her feet. "Mrs. Groves, you haven't slept, have you? Couldn't I stand by while you catch a nap? I could call you if anything happened—"

"Any nursing experience?"

"No."

"Then I'm afraid not. But thank you for the offer. We've had a lot of morbidly curious would-be visitors this morning. You're the first who wanted to do anything. Don't worry; my husband will relieve me after a while. He's a doctor."

"Oh, you're the missionaries. I met him. Mrs. Groves, when—when your patient wakes up—" She was going to ask her to give the fat girl a cheery message from her, but the girl didn't know her name. "I'm sorry to have troubled you," she said to the nurse and turned back to her car.

This time she knocked on Mona Greer's door.

The writer was patrician in an ice-blue hostess coat, and perfectly groomed. "Well, little one," she smiled.

"I came to say good morning and try to scrounge a cup of coffee. I don't think I can face the mob in the diner."

"Very sensible, darling. Come in." She drew her in by the hand, and Joan noticed with cold objectivity that she did not shrink and stiffen at the woman's touch, as she did at a man's. When it was a woman it wasn't real; you were just playing and knew it. You couldn't be trapped into love and dependence and slavery.

Mona rang for service.

"Coffee and a coddled egg and dry toast," she told the waiter. "Little one?" Joan nodded. "For two. Why isn't this thing moving?"

"'Deed I don't know, ma'am. Maybe we waiting for snowplows."

"Snowplows! Good God! How long will that take?"

"Not very long, ma'am," the waiter soothed. "Western division's got lots of snowplows. That be all, ma'am?"

"Yes, that's all."

Mona fumed. "Little one, have you ever noticed the disposition of sea captains and railroad men to regard all passengers as mentally defective?" A brilliant smile broke through. "But we'll have more time together, won't we? Will you like that?"

"Of course, Mona," she said, smiling. And she would. More time with this brilliant, amusing woman whose horizons were as wide as the world was exactly what she would like. Had she thought last night she felt tenderly towards Boyce? It hadn't been tenderness; it must have been contempt for a grubby little man whose touch was frightening.

"This will amuse you, Mona," she said. "Mr. Boyce tried to make love to me last night."

Mona Greer's eyes were hooded like a serpent's. "Indeed?"

Joan told her the story, and it was amusing. It was a tainted, poisoned version of what had happened. It was the way Joan remembered it for Mona, the way she wanted to remember it for herself. She tried hard to believe it, and succeeded for minutes at a time. Boyce had been a ruttish, bumbling fool. She had been cool and amused. He had stammered incoherently, but her prose had been stately and impeccable. She had, finally, tired of the game and left him stammering in the dark.

"Well done, darling," Mona told her warmly, patting her hand. "I'm proud of you."

The waiter knocked and was admitted with their breakfasts. His hand rattled the coffeepots and dishes, and he fumbled the change three times.

Mona drilled him with a look. "What's the matter with you?"

"Nothing, ma'am," he said, sweating. "Nothing at all. Them snowplows'll be right along. Like I said, Western division got lots of—"

"Oh," said Mona Greer, and paused. "So that's the way it is. Listen to me. My little friend and I are feeling hungrier than we thought. I want you to bring us about four dozen hard-boiled eggs. And a cooked ham. And a couple of loaves of bread. Things like that."

"Ma'am," he shrilled, "I cain' do anything like that—"

"Nonsense. You probably have more than that tucked away in your bunk right now. Here." There was a hundred-dollar bill in her hand.

"Man!" he said, staring at it. And then, collectedly: "Of course, ma'am, I'd have to split with the diner steward—"

"How much, damn you? Stop the Uncle Tom crap."

"Okay, lady," he said. "Gimme another big boy like that and it be worth my while."

She whipped out another hundred-dollar bill and handed them to him. "If you cross me up," she said evenly, "I'll tell the company you made a pass at me."

"I won't cross you up," he said contemptuously, "and you don't scare me worth a damn, lady. I be back with the stuff in an hour. 'Scuse me." Leaning against the wall, he yanked off one shoe and put the bills in it, folded small. He worked the foot back into the shoe and left.

"Little one," Mona Greer said to Joan, "it's a lucky thing you're in good hands." She stared through the window at the driving, wind-whipped snow. Already it was beginning to drift against the stalled train. Underfoot the futile thrumming vibration of the locomotive still sounded.

"It's going to get cold," Mona Greer said thoughtfully.

"Do you really think we're stranded?" asked Joan incredulously.

"That's not the point, little one," Mona said serenely. "The point is that if we're stranded you and I are going to be stranded with what little comforts we can arrange for ourselves. Ring the maid, will you please? We shall want some extra blankets against the winter wind." Joan rang, thinking it was exciting and interesting. There was a small doubt about the blankets that she expressed.

"Darling, you're so deliriously dumb I could kiss you," Mona laughed. "Do you think I give a rambling damn about anybody else going short on blankets? Do you think the maid will give a damn when she sees a hundred-dollar bill all for her? Do you think anybody else bright enough to arrange these elementary precautions would give a damn about us going short on blankets?"

She was right about the maid, who lusted after a hundred-dollar bill with her eyes and brought them, in three furtive trips, one dozen of the thin, grey pullman blankets. She had been right about the waiter. He brought them eggs, bread, half of a big boiled ham and cans of evaporated milk.

"How's it going?" Mona asked him coldly.

"Passengers beginning to wonder. Ol' conductor lying his head off to 'em. Won't be able to lie much longer. Me, I'm gonna go hide in a corner somewheres until this thing blows over."

CHAPTER XXI

SNOW

The railroad's public relations director stumped into his oak-paneled office, where the phone was already ringing. He picked it up without taking off his hat and said: "Lafferty here."

"This is Tom Hendricks, INS, Mr. Lafferty. What's the word on the Golden Gate Express?"

"I just got in, Mr. Hendricks. Okay if I call you back? When's your deadline?"

"The Breakfast Roundup gets out in twenty-five minutes."

"Okay, call you back."

He got his hat off and the phone rang again. It was the AP wanting to know about the Golden Gate Express. The Air Force had sent a plane over and spotted it drifted in at Raton Pass—

"Call you back."

While he was shucking his coat the New York Times bureau rang.

"Call you back."

"Take incoming calls and stall," he called to his secretary, and got on the other phone, checking with Chicago dispatcher, Denver dispatcher and Air Force Public Relations Officer—

It was bad; it was very bad. The Denver snowplows were on their way at a crawling two miles per hour, the nearest town was isolated by drifted roads and snapped phone wires, food and fuel would run out before the plows arrived—it was very bad.

He called Hendricks at the INS and put a smile in his voice. "Everything's under control, you can tell your clients. The train has halted, but there's nothing to be concerned over. There's ample food and fuel aboard and there will be no hardships. I see, incidentally, that this is the first episode of its kind in eighteen years. And you can tell the people that it probably won't happen again for another eighteen years."

He gave the same story to the AP, the Times and the UP, and then called Denver again.

"Listen," he told the Division Manager savagely. "You get that train dug out in six hours or write your resignation." He was a vice president of the corporation.

The Division Manager said: "It can't be done—"

"The hell with that talk! Do it!" He slammed the phone down and sat back, his arteries pounding. He thought of the haw-haw the airlines would give the rails, the word-of-mouth stories, the jokes. And of the people who might freeze or starve.

CHAPTER XXII

UNDER THE SKIN

Foreman was having an after-breakfast drink. The thrumming energy of the locomotive, running along the cars, made the bottle tremble in his hand.

It sounded different.

He corked the bottle precisely, opened his two-suiter and found his portable radio. Reception would be lousy in an all-metal car, he thought, lifting the lid and turning the compact set carefully for direction.

Mushily: "—KMOX, Denver, every hour on the hour. First, a bulletin from the wires of the United Press." Foreman allowed himself a professional sneer. The UP and their bulletins, followed later by carefully-worded climbdowns from the "estimated casualties" or the "record-breaking damage." But listen: "Seventeen, that is seventeen, crack passenger trains are overdue at Colorado and Montana points as much as eight hours. Railroad officials said it is too early to say that some of these trains may be stranded by record-breaking snowdrifts in the mountains. But they admitted that this is always a possibility. Snowplows of the various lines are proceeding cautiously to clear drifted rights-of-way. Their crews report drifts up to twelve feet deep.

"Meanwhile, the vicious snowstorm that has been lashing the west for two days continues unabated." Foreman glanced out of the window. The snow had stopped falling. "Property damage and loss to herds on winter range is estimated at—"

The newsman closed down the lid of the portable with an uneasy feeling that he'd better save its batteries.

Do a story on this, he told himself. Get out the Remington Model Five, put in copy paper.

Snowbound—1

by Larry Foreman

World Wireless Staff Writer

Aboard Snowbound Golden Gate Express—A crack passenger train is stranded today by towering snowdrifts in Ratan Pass, Colorado.

And I'm aboard it writing this eyewitness account. At this time neither I nor anybody else on board knows what lies ahead. It may be prompt rescue by snowplows reported chugging our way. Or it may be an ordeal of several days on short rations—

Knock off it, newsman. The working press can cover this one. Stick to your horse wire and don't try to compete with the professionals.

Foreman took his drink at last, a long, deep one from the bottle.

He wandered back through the train, seeing and hearing with the cold, delusive clarity of a man who is one-third drunk and knows it. The pitch of things had changed. The holiday buzz of passengers, the querulousness of the middle-aged and the riotousness of the young had been shoved up a notch.

"I-da-wa-a-a-na!" shrieked a little girl in a coach seat, and her grim-faced mother fetched her a terrifying crack across the face. Her eyes were insane, peering every way—except through the window, at the white blanket over the scattered pines and rocks. The little girl's father yelled at the mother in Italian, and four raucous college boys yelled with laughter across the aisle, mocking him.

"Hey," said the father to them, icily. "What so funny you punks laugh?"

"You joost take-a it easy, Pop," one of the boys said, kindly enough, with an ambiguous hint of accent, and they laughed again.

The next car was compartments, drawing rooms, roomettes. An old man's head popped wildly through one of the doors. Around his stringy neck was a high collar and no tie. "Excuse me, young man," he said. "If you see the conductor would you be good enough to ask him to—"

From the compartment came a woman's quaver: "You go yourself, Harvey. I told you to go yourself, so you go yourself and don't try to pass the responsibility—"

The lined old face made a conciliatory grimace and disappeared.

In the vestibule the four sulky men from the Ordnance Corps were standing, being harangued by a thin eye-glassed boy in an enlisted man's uniform wearing Signal Corps braid and insignia and the circular Officer's Candidate School patch on his forearm.

"—I'm not in charge of you fellows," he was saying earnestly. "I'm just telling you what I think you ought to do and what I'm going to do. Seems we're going to be stuck here for a while, so what with our first-aid training and everything we ought to volunteer to the conductor to help out any way we can. What do you say?"

The corporal looked grave and said: "I'll tell you what I say." He threw back his head and yelled: "Go to hell, Jack!" and the four of them exploded into laughter.

"Ah'm gonna volunteer," one of them said stagily. "Ah'm gonna volunteer to take care of any left-over babes on this heah train, hey, Harold?"

The O.C.S. boy looked sick and hurried on, brushing past Foreman. Heads popped out along the corridor to stare at the noise.

"Hey, Mister," Foreman called to the boy. "Don't take it so—"

"The hell with you too, Jack," the O.C.S. boy said hysterically, and ducked into the washroom. First command, no doubt, Foreman thought dryly.

He weaved into the club car. The attendant had made the mistake of appearing before eleven o'clock opening time, and was under siege.

"Boy," a blue serge suit was telling him, "I'm a lawyer specializing in interstate commerce. Giant corporations pay me up to ten thousand dollars for a single opinion. And you dare to stand there with your bare teeth hanging out of your black face and tell me I'm a liar!"

"Nossir!" cried the attendant. "Didn't say that at all! But the rule—"

"Didn't I just tell you that acts of God suspend the rulebook on the serving of interstate booze and refreshments? Didn't I?"

"That's right, judge! Make him open up!" clamored from the early-rising lushes. "Don't let him call you a liar!"

"—didn't say that at all, gentlemen—"

"What's going on here, Bunker?" It was the conductor: an ancient, miniature bulldog and suddenly the most important person in the limited little world they lived in.

The attendant tried to explain, but his besiegers had lost interest in the game. Strangely respectful of the little old man, they were asking: "What's the pitch, conductor? When do we get rolling again? We going to be very late into Frisco?"

The conductor lifted his arms oratorically for silence. "Gentlemen," he said, "There's nothing to worry about. I'm sure division snowplows are on the way and we'll be dug out in a few hours."

"You're sure," shot the man who said he was a lawyer. "That means you don't know."

"Bunker," the conductor said to the attendant, "open the bar for the gentlemen."

A sudden quiet descended on the middle-aged group.

"Well?" said the conductor testily. "Isn't that what you wanted?" He stumped away from them in the silence. Silently they turned to the bar.

The lawyer finally said: "It doesn't look too good, is my guess. Double Scotch, boy; water on the side."

Somebody—Foreman recognized Loober, the insurance man—muttered: "Guess I miss the convention. Same for me, boy."

"You said you were a lawyer, mister. (Rye-gingerale.) Do we have any kind of a claim—"

"Not a damn bit. All the railroad contracts to do is try to get you to your destination—"

"The damnedest thing I ever heard of!"

"Sue if you want to, friend. Meanwhile have one with me."

The business-suited middle-aged took the edge off with a couple of quick ones and then scattered generally with glasses in their hands to the biggest, deepest chairs, talking quietly, unhappily and seeming to make a point of not glancing through the windows. The windows were drifting in on one side. Foreman thought he felt the cold bite through the aluminum and steel wall.

Hundreds of yards up the track the twin diesel-electric locomotives made a final convulsive effort that shivered down the length of the train to the club car, and then changed their tune. They no longer roared with effort to shove through the tons of snow, but purred and grumbled on a minimum turnover.

"That's that," somebody in the club car said. "End of the line."

"It's unbelievable," somebody else said wonderingly. "In this day and age—of course they'll have us dug out in a few hours."

"What price those railroad ads knocking the airlines now?"

"'Go by rail, forget the weather, arrive refreshed.'"

Ragged, worried laughter.

Foreman watched, brooding, from behind a drink, as the attendant walked with a tray to one of the big chairs. A grey-haired, red-faced man intercepted him. "That must be mine, boy."

"Like hell it is," said a fat man from the big chair. "Bring it here, boy." The attendant froze half-way between them. The grey-haired man got up, calmly took the drink from the tray and dropped a dollar bill on it, and returned to his seat at one of the little tables. The attendant saw the fat man get up grimly. He scurried back behind his bar and began polishing glasses.

"All right, wise guy," the fat man said. "Give it here."

The grey-haired man looked at him speculatively and put the glass to his lips. The fat man, with a roundhouse swing, knocked it from his face. It crashed against the floor. Seemingly before it hit the two men were a swearing, panting tangle of limbs.

Foreman dove in and grabbed at a flailing arm, he didn't know whose. Another arm promptly caught him a clip in the nose, and he let go, swearing. Half a dozen bystanders finally got the two pulled apart, and they stood like bulls, glaring.

The lawyer lectured them ferociously: "If you two goons can't hold your liquor the least you can do is get out of here and not bother people who can. Any more trouble and I'll call the conductor. You may not happen to know it, but he's legally able to arrest you and turn you over to the police at the next stop."

"When's that going to be, mister?" the grey-haired man asked softly, still panting. He shook himself loose and the fat man stepped back, quailing. The grey-haired man didn't even look at him. He walked to the bar and told the attendant: "Boy, give me a dozen of those little bottles. Put 'em in a bag or something."

"'Deed I'm sorry, sir, but they're for drinking in the car heah, only—"

"Didn't you hear what I said, you stupid ape?"

The attendant's face froze. "Gettum right away, sir." He went back into his little galley and didn't come out again.

For a long minute and a half the conversation was sparse and strained, and the grey-haired man stood at the bar shifting from foot to foot. At last he said, loudly, to all of them: "The hell with this." He put a ten-dollar bill on the bar, went behind it and scooped a dozen train bottles into his pockets while they stared. He stalked from the car unmolested.

Bill Loober said to Foreman: "That guy has the right idea. It may be a long time between drinks." The insurance man looked belligerently around, went to the bar, filled his own pockets and left—a five.

The panic was on. The business-suited middle-aged raided the bar with jokes and excuses and a pretense of payment at first that rapidly disappeared.

Foreman sat alone, watching them jostle and shoulder each other, half-gloating, half-ashamed, thoroughly surprised at themselves. He knew what they were thinking and feeling. He had been to the wars and he knew looting when he saw it.

He watched with quiet, drunken interest, the churning mob around the bar. Looting was a swift, downward path, a rapid shedding of civilized inhibitions about property. First you realized the rules were off. Then you took what you wanted. And finally you got silly and destructive.

The fat man emitted a drunken war-whoop and flung a bottle of club soda at one of the highly colored Koda-chrome blowups that decorated the club car. The bottle didn't smash but the picture glass protecting the Koda-chrome from smudgy fingers did, and tinkled on the carpeted floor.

"For Christ's sake, man!" somebody yelled. It scared them all, and the crowd evaporated swiftly through the door leaving Foreman in sole possession of the field.

The college boys from the coach car bucked their way through the stream and stood, bewildered, in the vestibule, staring at Foreman.

"Somebody said they were giving away liquor—" one of them said to him uncertainly. "What kind of a gag—?"

"No gag at all, boy," Foreman said kindly. He got up. "I guess there's a crowd and the trainmen on your heels?"

They nodded.

"Then there's no time to lose. I'll show you how an old pro works this deal." He went behind the bar, which was cleaned out. "Watch this one." He kicked the galley door right at the keyhole; there was a splintering noise and it swung open, pretty as a picture. Under the sandwich counter honeycombed cases of train bottles were stacked. He filled his pockets and said: "Pitch in, gentlemen." Incredulously, they did, as passengers began to boil in, chattering.

He worked his way through, shoving politely, glimpsing the distorted faces of the conductor and trainmen and car attendant who were futilely yelling nothing that could be heard.

Foreman got clear of the mob. Its after reaches consisted of bewildered passengers who didn't quite know what was going on and were trying to explain it to each other. He dropped, chuckling, into a leather seat in a smoking room two cars back. A woman put her head between the green curtains. "You came from back there," she said accusingly. "What on earth's going on? Is it an announcement?"

"Lady," Foreman said, pretending to be shocked and almost feeling it, "this is the boys' room."

"Oh," she said impatiently, and the head disappeared.

She felt it in the air, the newsman thought. That was another thing that vanished when there were no cops to pull you in. God almighty, what boils beneath the skin of our societies! Wound the skin with war or a freak of the weather like this and what gushes out is the true nature of man: plunder and rape and—he felt an odd coldness—and, of course, murder.

He pulled one of the little bottles from his pocket and regarded it carefully: a square-faced miniature of a square-faced bottle of a famous brand of Scotch. People collected the cute little things. He wrenched off the metal-foil, brittle cap and drank the two ounces of whisky in two matter-of-fact swallows.

I think, he told himself precisely, I'll see how Greer and Lundberg are getting along.

CHAPTER XXIII

SNOW

Officer Candidate Milton F. Martinson writhed at the thought of the soldiers' derision. And he knew what he had to do.

He walked through the train until he found the conductor, who was the center of an irascible knot of passengers. Politely he said to him: "Conductor, I'm willing to go and get help from the nearest town. I have inclement-weather clothes in my dufflebag. If you'll just give me an idea of where to head—"

The group fell silent and the conductor stared fixedly at him. "Better not, soldier," he said at last. "Rush City ought to be north of here a few miles, but you'd better wait for them to come to us."

"Let the kid go, conductor," somebody said. "He can take care of himself, can't you, kid? They learn all about it in the army."

Martinson flushed under "kid" but said: "Certainly I can take care of myself. I think it's your duty, conductor, to—"

There was a clamor of agreement. They wouldn't go themselves, of course, but they'd be delighted to send somebody else.

"All right," the conductor snapped.

Martinson was already wearing G.I. long-handled underwear and olive-drab wool. He got into his sweater, field jacket and overcoat, double socks and galoshes, balaclava helmet and gloves. He was streaming sweat in the heated car when the conductor opened the vestibule door and the train door for him and a curious crowd wished him good luck.

"Tell 'em to bring some booze, kid," a heavily humorous man said. "I missed out on my share."

"Send a doctor first thing," a woman told him. "Dr. Groves is ready to collapse and there's a girl going to have a baby—"

He nodded and plunged into the cold.

At first it did not seem cold. The snow no longer fell and there was no wind to speak of. It was the "still cold" of which he had been warned; the cold that catches you unawares and leaves ears and fingers and nose wax-white. But he was wrapped well enough—

He floundered through a foot of powdery snow on the lee side of the train and plunged down the embankment. He fumbled out his compass and dropped it with his mittened fingers. Three tries to scoop it out of the snow failed; he pulled the glove with his teeth and groped bare-handed in a small drift for the compass. Still with one hand bare, he opened it and sighted north to a distinctive crag, put it away, put on his glove and began to march for the crag.

Quite suddenly he realized that he was in trouble. The air burned in his lungs, the odd coldness of his hands, the creeping cold in his toes despite the double socks, the burning of his nose—the very sweat was freezing on his body.

The insidious dry cold had penetrated five layers of wool before he had marched a hundred yards to the distinctive crag. And his hand was on fire.

His feet were without sensation, and they betrayed him. He fell in the snow, face-down. "Son of a bitch," he mumbled into the snow. "Get out of here." He heaved himself to his knees; the pressure on his burning hand was agony. People were yelling at him from the train; he couldn't make out what. He knelt in the snow shading his eyes to stare at the train and saw grotesque bundled figures heading his way. Then the cold gripped him and he couldn't even see.

Later he felt that he was being carried and he heard screams:

"He's frozen! He's frozen! We're all going to die out here!"

"Shut up, lady. He'll be all right if you'll get the hell out of the way—"

"Rub him with snow—"

"No, you crazy bastard! You want to kill him?"

"Somebody get that doctor—"

"We're all going to freeze out here!"

"Shut up, lady!"

He listened as if to a radio show. He was no longer an actor; he had done his best. And as usual it had not been good enough.

CHAPTER XXIV

TURTLES

Pilar Mackenzie, a fat girl far from the Galapagos Islands, lay and sweated and listened to her heart. False labor, the pleasant doctor and his peppery wife had called it. If that was false labor, she didn't want to encounter the real thing—not that she had any choice. After maturity, every twenty-eight days an ovum descended. Given an opportunity, a sperm cell would lash its way upstream like a spawning salmon to meet and penetrate the ovum. Within minutes the one cell became two, the two four, the four eight, and in two hundred and fifty days, give or take a couple of weeks, you gave birth even it it killed you.

Which it would.

She listened to her heart, wrecked and sputtering from the false labor pains, and pondered on a theory that once had amused her. It was that the human race consists not of the clothes-wearing, house-building, money-making organisms ordinarily called people but of their sperm cells and ova. The clothes-wearers were brushed aside as transitional forms useful to the sperm, but with no reality or continuity of their own except as far as they produced and protected more sperms and ova. The theory was amusing no longer. She had vowed from the moment the first inadequate local doctor made his unconfirmed diagnosis that she would not give in to anger or hate, but her defenses were crumbling. You got tricked into it by boredom and glands, she angrily thought. With no serious intentions you played around and then something extremely serious happened. There had been no pleasure in it for her; eating a chocolate cream would have provided a finer sensory experience. Nevertheless, anticipating no pleasure, experiencing none, aware that something awfully bad might come of it, she had gone ahead. Now it was two hundred and fifty days later and she was dying of it, apparently. There seemed to be nothing in it for anybody or anything except the human germ cells which met in her without her awareness of their meeting. Arturo got no pleasure from it, she was sure. He had muttered curses against her fat and her clumsiness and later on he had lost his job on suspicion and had been sent back to the poverty-stricken mainland hamlet he came from. No pleasure there at all. Her parents were far from pleased indeed. After a dreadful quarrel in which she was the pawn, her mother locked herself in and prayed; her father locked himself in and drank.

"You will not have the child here," her father said at last, and gave her money and his sister's address in Baltimore. "For God's sake, child, pray to be forgiven," said her mother, and gave her the principal part of her own old dowry, an old-fashioned necklace of Brazilian emeralds.

She sold the necklace at Humpp's in Honolulu, the steamer's first stop, and half its considerable price went in the first month to a great midwestern clinic and its staff which at last pronounced that the odds against her survival were a hundred to one.

So Pilar Mackenzie never got to the aunt in Baltimore. The rest of the price of the necklace had been spent to buy her what she perhaps had looked for, foolishly, in Arturo's arms. She stood for most of one day on the observation platform of the Empire State Building in New York, savoring the queer thought that men had built this extraordinarily tall stepladder. She saw legitimate plays for the first time in her life, and it was her good luck that she arrived at the height of the most brilliant theatrical season in years. She laughed and wept unashamedly in the audience, loving wonderful people named O'Casey, Rodgers and Hammerstein, Mary Martin, Oenslager, all the writers, actors, composers and designers who could make little worlds for her that lasted two hours and a lifetime.

She ate, too. Dear God, how she ate of what New York had to spread before her! She used to think she knew Chinese cookery, for the cook on the estancia was a Chinese Chileno, but then she met the real thing in New York and ate her way almost in rapture through hours of subtle blends, this flavor played against that, this texture played against that. They came to know her too in the small Italian restaurants, and she came to love the Italians' tender chicken and veal stewed gently for half a day with peppers and onions and spices she never had tasted before. It was in these places she learned that Chianti, though rough on the tongue and metallic in taste, could be a noble wine when it was properly used.

In sukiyaki restaurants she watched happily while a little waitress in kimono and huge sash arranged the raw vegetables and thin slices of red beef in the pan of bubbling sauce that sat on the little stove at the table. For twenty minutes you could study the artful arrangement of the cooking pieces and smell their heavenly steam, and then eating them came almost as an anticlimax, but not quite. She read about, and sighed for, cha no yu, the Japanese custom (or minor religion, or art, or philosophy) of ceremonial tea drinking, but in the time she had she could not learn of any Tea Master in the country who might instruct her.

They came to know her a little, and respect her greatly, at a Long Island restaurant conceded to be the only American exponent of the great international cuisine; there she met blue trout, truffled poularde, duck with orange, the great cheeses, the classic sauces, the singing wines of the world.

There was music for her, too. She chose to bypass the great ones, Callas, de los Angeles, Monteux, Stokowski, Heifetz. Instead she attended debuts, afternoon and evening recitals in the Carnegie Chamber Music Hall where youngsters laid it on the line for the first time in public. They were sopranos from Texas, baritones from Duluth, pianists from Brooklyn, fiddlers from everywhere, and they were laying four or five thousand dollars on the line and praying that they'd rate a favorable review from a second-string critic, praying that they'd find one small crack in the wall between them and fame. Pilar Mackenzie bought her tickets and sat among the scattering of critics, teachers, fellow-students and relations of the debutant to listen with pleasure and applaud loudly. Pierre Monteux could get along nicely without her, and perhaps she was helping the debutantes a little.

Her money and her time were running out when she read that the San Francisco Symphony Orchestra was going to present a weeklong Monteverdi festival. She wanted to hear some more Monteverdi, so without thinking much about it she wired for tickets, checked out of her small midtown hotel and boarded a train. She had left in her purse forty-four dollars and in her life—how many days?

She felt cold, and wondered if it was the cold of the Rockies or the cold of death coming over her. Apologetically she had asked for another blanket and the pleasant doctor had provided one. It wasn't enough, but something kept her from asking for more.

Her heart was skipping again.

CHAPTER XXV

SAD STORIES

Boyce sat forlornly in his half of the seat, not knowing whether he wished or didn't wish Joan were in her half. Behind him there was a buzzing confusion from which the words clearly came: "—free drinks in the club car!"

He turned and saw an excited young man in the rear vestibule, surrounded by a dozen passengers talking at once. They melted through the vestibule and curious men got up to follow them asking one another: "What did the kid say? What was that about?"

Boyce thought of following, but didn't. The hell with their free drinks. Drinks were for people who didn't know what they wanted. He knew what he wanted. It was just the breaks that it was forever beyond his reach.

It was getting colder. Mechanically he hauled down his suitcase and got out his overcoat to drape around his shoulders. Damn nuisance—they'd have the heat up again in a few minutes and he'd just have to pack it again. But at least it would kill some time that he would surely spend otherwise brooding about the impossible that had seemed so real a handful of hours ago.

Joan and he somewhere away from the reeking air of Chicago, someplace where it was sunlit like the southwest, and some kids, boys or girls, he didn't care which, and a job. He'd work like a dog for them and be happy to—real work, not outguessing a padded expense account, not joking a debt-plagued housewife into buying a more expensive carpet than she could afford, not cooking up phony sales, not clawing at the advertising meetings for more inches than Major Appliances or Furniture as if your life depended on it.

Peggy, his wife, seemed very far away and unreal compared to the blonde girl he had known for a little more than a day. Maybe these were the dangerous forties. Maybe the dangerous forties were no joke or problem to be calmly handled according to the psychology columns of the slick-paper women's magazines. Maybe the dangerous forties of the American husband were exactly this sickening realization that he had been trapped by a lying stranger and that this was his very last chance to struggle free—and that he had lost it.

He could, he thought savagely, glance at a room and tell Mrs. Whoozis to the dollar what it would cost her in taupe broadloom wall to wall—and why taupe broadloom was less dashing than the more expensive sculptured Wilton that they were laying in so many of the smart Gold Coast apartments these days. But he couldn't tell the girl he loved that he loved her and that she had to love him or make his life less than nothing, a nagging nuisance just below the level of pain.

The porter worked his way down the aisle, grinning, shaking his head, shrugging his shoulders at people who tried to question him. He stopped and studied the baggage rack above Boyce's head. "'Scuse me, suh, would you please show me which are your bags? I got to move the lady's into the other lady's compartment." His face was absolutely blank.

"I guess you guys have seen just about everything," Boyce said uncontrollably.

"Yes, suh," the porter said, dead-pan.

Boyce showed him his bags and Joan's. He took Joan's bags in one great load and staggered down the aisle. The rug man got up and followed him, his overcoat flapping around him. He let the porter go in and timidly rapped on the door.

Joan opened it and said coolly: "Hello, there."

"Hello," he said. "If there's anything I can do—"

Her eyebrows lifted. "You're very kind," she said. There was an inquiring murmur in the compartment. Joan turned and said into it: "It's Mr. Boyce, Mona."

"Ask him in for cocktails—later," came the voice more clearly. "We take care of our own, don't we, darling?"

Joan smiled impersonally at the rug man. "We're crowded now with the porter," she said. "But I'd love to have you in for a—a sundowner." She turned again: "Is that what you called it, Mona?"

"Only in the tropics, darling. My, what a draft!"

"About six?" Joan smiled at Boyce, and closed the door. And her smile had had something crazy about it. From her eyes there seemed to scream a plea: Get me out of this! For God's sake, get me out of here!

Boyce stood in the corridor, bemused, as the porter bustled out, wearing a grin that clicked off as he closed the door. He looked at Boyce for a moment and hurried to his cubbyhole at the end of the car. His annuciator board must have dropped a number. A moment later he popped out again wearily, squared his shoulders, and trudged to another door and rapped politely.

An old woman opened the door a grudging few inches and snarled: "You took long enough, I must say. It's getting cold in here. You tell the conductor or the engineer or whoever is responsible that Mr. and Mrs.

Brining insist on a reasonable temperature being maintained. Mr. Brining suffers from asthma and diabetes. Do you understand that? Asthma and diabetes. Be sure to tell him that."

"Yes, ma'am," said the porter sympathetically. "I surely will, this minute. Is that all, ma'am?"

"That's all, boy." The door slammed shut and the porter's shoulders slumped as he trudged back to his cubbyhole.

Weaving down the aisle came Foreman, his pockets bulging.

"Hello, Boyce," he said, and jerked his thumb at the closed compartment door. "They receiving?"

"No," Boyce grunted. "Cocktails at six."

"Booze. Fine. Come on-a my house, Boyce. Have a cocktail with me at eleven or whatever the hell time it is. We can listen to whatever crap they're dishing out on the radio."

"You have a radio? I never thought of that. Maybe we can find out—"

"The hell we can. I've covered hassles like this. All the radio will do is quote the railroad public relations men. All the public relations men will do is say everything's going to be okay in a couple of hours."

The lights dimmed perceptibly as they marched down the corridor, and stayed dim.

"What's that?" Boyce demanded irritably.

"This is a diesel-electric, friend. Diesels generate electricity and electricity makes the wheels go around, supplies heat and supplies light. I guess they're skimping on the light to give us more heat longer."

They were passing through the fabric-covered tunnel-link between cars as he spoke, and the cold cut like a knife.

They got where they were going, and Foreman collapsed morosely onto his berth and after a moment began to go through his pockets and methodically set train bottles of liquor on the shelf. "What'll you have?" he demanded. "We seem to have acquired a mixed batch of bourbon, Scotch—white and black label—blended rye and for God's sake a bottle of Cointreau."

"Where'd you get them?" asked Boyce, astonished.

"There was a slight moral breakdown in the club car. I and about a dozen respectable businessmen ran amuck and pillaged the stocks. Rape and murder are still in the cards," he said broodingly.

"You're pretty drunk."

"You're pretty too, Boyce, but let's not start that. There's enough of it going on."

"For God's sake, lay off me!"

Foreman paused and seemed surprised. "I'm sorry," he said. "I don't know what the hell's wrong with me. Nothing but fights, fights, fights since

I got aboard—even with that jerk of a lieutenant. For no reason at all there I was practically begging him to take a swing at me." He shook his head.

"You're drinking too much," Boyce said doggedly. "You work in a higher-pressure line than I do, but business is business and I've got more experience than you. I'm older and I missed the war. Liquor isn't going to do you a damn bit of good. I've seen them come and go for, God, it must be eighteen years now. They start like you and they wind up in the gutter unless they knock off the stuff. If you want to get anywhere, if you want to be respected, you've got to control it and not let it control you."

Foreman asked, with real interest: "You don't believe any of that crap, do you?"

Boyce said wearily, after a pause: "I guess not. Not today, anyway. I've believed it for eighteen years, though. And what did it get me?"

Foreman laughed harshly. "Come, let us sit upon the ground together and tell sad stories of the death of salesmen. Do you know when I decided I was going to get the hell out of the news business? When I looked one day at my typewriter and saw that I was writing the obituary of a horse. Man O' War, old Big Red, but still a horse. What kind of way is that to spend your life?"

Boyce said: "So you quit the news business and lived happily ever after. Congratulations. I wish I had your nerve."

Foreman didn't seem to have heard him. He was staring straight ahead and saying: "—and now I can't get out. Not ever. They've got me for life." There was panic in his eyes. Boyce had the sudden, startled feeling that below the drinking, the kidding and the cynicism, this panic was Foreman's eternal bedrock.

He cleared his throat. "You said you have a radio—"

"Yeah. Sure. What the hell was I talking about?" He got the portable from his suitcase and opened and oriented it.

Static sputtered and then there was music. Reception was poor, but it was unmistakably the Bing Crosby record of White Christmas. Foreman looked through the window and grinned humorlessly. "Liquor's dying in me," he said. "I think I'll let it die." He got out his overcoat, a bulky fleece-lined beaver-collared storm coat.

"You're really ready," Boyce said, staring at it.

"I guess every Chicago legman has one like this," Foreman said comfortably. "You go out at three A.M. on a February morning to cover a fire or a collision on the Drive and if you haven't got one you get one as soon as the shops open. Dentistry can wait, Household Finance Corp. can wait. You get a storm coat."

"It must be an exciting life," Boyce said wistfully.

"It stinks on dry ice," Foreman said. "Here's a 'cast."

The radio was saying blurrily something about giant snowplows and Air Force spotter planes and record-breaking drifts and record-breaking cattle losses and Federal disaster aid rushed through Congress and: "Here is a late bulletin. The Golden Gate Express, overdue Chicago-San Francisco streamliner, has been sighted by Air Force spotter planes from Chanute Air Force Base drifted in at Raton Pass. Nearest settlement is Rush City, some eight miles north of the stalled streamliner. Tricky mountain air currents made it impossible for the Air Force planes to land, but emergency rations were dropped. The crack streamliner is the target of giant railroad snowplows crawling through the record-breaking drifts on a mission of mercy. Phone and telegraph lines to Rush City are down, but—" the rest was static.

Boyce looked wonderingly at Foreman. "What was that about emergency rations?"

"Air Force P.R.O. stuff. Sure they dropped them. Did you notice he didn't say where?" He slammed the lid of the radio shut furiously. "That butterball that was going to have the baby," he said. "Maybe she can use this goddamn coat if the cold gets any worse."

"Why—that's a very nice thought. And a very good idea."

"Okay, okay. Come on."

They went out into a steady flow of passengers heading for the diner, not running, but walking a good stiff heel-and-toe, casting sidelong glances, not letting themselves be passed. First luncheon call wouldn't be for a half-hour yet, but half the train was congesting the corridor. The funny-looking little dining car attendant was exhorting them: "Please, ladies and gentlemen, there will be enough for all! This it totally unnecessary! You'll simply make yourselves uncomfortable by having to stand around—"

They were paying him absolutely no attention. They wouldn't, any of them, let him hold them up a single second because then they might number 167 in line instead of number 165. Plain on every face was fear that there would be exactly one serving of lunch too few.

The lights were dimmer still as they drifted with the tide of passengers.

"This is it," Boyce said, and knocked.

Dr. Groves opened the door. "Hello there," he said cordially. And then his face fell as he got a blast of Foreman's breath.

"Don't tell me off please, doctor," the newsman said hastily, shrugging out of the stormcoat. "I was wondering if the little lady could use this."

"She certainly can," the doctor-preacher said, beaming. "You're the answer to a prayer, sir. All the spare blankets and a few that aren't spares seem to have evaporated. I'm afraid some people are hoarding and the maids and porters must be in on it, too. They just look blank and say they don't know anything about—"

"She'll die, won't she?" Foreman interrupted.

Dr. Groves said quietly: "I think so. In view of that, do you wish to withdraw the offer of your coat?"

Foreman thought incredulously: He's got me mixed up with some superstitious peasant he converted somewhere. He's got me mixed up with a nice, sanitary white-collar professional young man who never saw a stiff that wasn't laid out and painted for a funeral. He doesn't know my arches were high and my eardrums unperforated and that therefore I made the long journey through ZI, through ComZ, to the line. That after one particular three-week spell in a defensive position I went way back, two whole miles, hundreds of yards behind the division artillery, with messages for Regiment and spent the night there at Regiment in sybaritic luxury. There was a chow line, hot food and non-instant coffee made with water that had really boiled. There was a stable, only partially demolished by shelling, to sleep in. There was a litter to sleep on! A springy canvas litter with legs! It smelled strongly for it was one of the litters used by the Graves Registration Section to collect bodies, but he hadn't given it a moment's thought. In the peace and quiet back there, way behind the artillery, he had even taken off his boots for the night...

"That's all right," he said to the doctor. "It won't bother me at all."

"Good," said the doctor. And then, very reluctantly, he added: "Foreman?"

"Yes?"

"I don't pretend to know the first thing about drunkenness. There are theories. Down at Texas State University they say it's biochemical. Up at Yale they say it's psychogenic. All I know is that the United States is having a rather severe epidemic of it right now. It's been worse; in the 1840's there was a strong possibility that drunkenness was going to cripple the country as a whole, but somehow it didn't happen. The point is, Foreman, that I feel like making an educated guess about you. I think you're the sort of fellow who's a good candidate to make the triple play. Alcoholism to nephritis to apoplexy."

"With all respect, doctor, mind your own business, will you?"

"Very well," said the doctor, with neither insult nor disappointment showing on his face. He heard a groan from behind the compartment door and said: "Excuse me." He took the coat, mysteriously held up two fingers in a V-for-victory sign, and popped back into the compartment. The door closed to the sound of another groan of immense visceral effort.

"V for victory?" Foreman marveled.

"Two fingers' dilation of the cervix, sergeant," a woman snapped. It was the lieutenant's red-head.

"Oh—hello," Foreman said. "How did you know and what does it mean?"

"Every woman knows about it. Doctors and nurses do that in the hospital to keep the mother-to-be guessing or something. Four fingers is it."

"You mean the baby's on its way?"

"That's what I mean, sergeant. The cervix dilates to four centimeters and then second-stage labor begins and the baby gets born. Do you know the doctor? I've got to talk to him." Hysteria edged her voice.

Junkie stuff. She wouldn't have started the trip without enough to carry her through, and a safety margin. She couldn't possibly have used up all her fixes; they weren't that much overdue. She was scared—just plain scared that she'd run short. She was going to con or coax the doctor out of whatever she could—

"Did you know he's a preacher?" Foreman asked carefully. "A medical missionary? And a shrewd, tough baby with an even shrewder, tougher wife who acts as his nurse?"

"Oh, God," she said, and looked sick. She wasn't even dismayed that he had seen through her, or that Boyce was listening in bewilderment. She hurried down the corridor, distractedly.

"Now what was that all about?" the rug man asked.

"We were just kidding around," Foreman said.

"I'm not convinced."

"I can't help that."

The luncheon chimes began to bong, plenty early.

"I guess," Foreman said groping wildly for a change of subject, "they figure on running that crowd through as fast as possible."

"I guess so. Think I'll get in line. You coming along?"

"I'll find a sweater or two to put on. I'll see you."

They parted, Boyce hurt at being shut out of some cryptic byplay and Foreman sorry that Boyce was hurt and glad he had an out.

The red-head was reclining on his berth when he got back to the compartment.

"I thought I left the door locked," he said.

"You did, sergeant. The porter had a key and I had a dollar. It was as simple as that. But you can lock the door now if you don't feel safe."

"I feel a hell of a lot safer with it unlocked. What can I do for you?"

She crossed her legs nicely and said: "Sergeant, don't you read anything at all? The last three runaway best-sellers have been about N.C.O.s making love to officers' wives."

He grinned humorlessly. "After the N.C.O.s steal a few jolts of M from the doctor's little black bag for the officers' wives?"

She licked her lips, suddenly thin and pale, but smiled the standard low-lidded smile that passes for sexual invitation in the movies and elsewhere. "After or before, sergeant. Try me? I'm good ..."

Hot hunger overcame him for this calculating slut. Corruption knows corruption, he thought again. She's all I rate; I'm poison now to a clean kid. "You'd better be," he said half-sullenly, and locked the door.

CHAPTER XXVI

SNOW

Mrs. Groves plowed through the crowd like a small tornado. "Where is he?" she demanded. "I'm the nurse." She displayed her husband's black doctor's bag.

They gave way, and she saw the boy, still bundled up, his face beet-red except for his nose, which was a dead, unhealthy white. She began to strip his outer clothes off and muttered: "God help him!" when she saw the right hand.

"The people who brought him in," she said, not looking up as she wound a dressing on the hand. "Are they all right?"

The tall trainman said: "Yes, ma'am. We kept moving and we had more on than him—"

"Good. Help me with his boots, will you?"

The toes were in bad shape; double socks had helped.

She straightened up. "Somebody should watch him. Bring him some food. And find me if there's any change ..."

The boy stirred and groaned.

Mrs. Groves thought: He'll be screaming in a minute. Decisively she prepared a morphine sulphate hypo and shot it into his arm. She didn't approve of indiscriminate drugging; it could lead to serious consequences for the patient. But the nervous crowd was on the edge of panic. If she let the boy scream with pain and fear, there might be a stampede.

She pulled her coat around her shoulders. Cold was beginning to leak into the train... the kind of cold that had seared the boy's face and hand and feet like fire.

And she trotted back down the car to return the doctor's bag to her husband. The Mackenzie woman might be giving birth this very minute...

CHAPTER XXVII
OF COURSE THE FRENCH

"They're ringing first call for lunch," Joan said doubtfully to Mona Greer. "Perhaps it wasn't necessary ..."

"Luncheon is one thing, darling," Mona said derisively. "Dinner's another. Especially when supplies for it were to be loaded at Phoenix. Now help me pin this blanket over the window. It's cooling off fast in here and that will help. And I think we'd better try some of la chauffage centrale francaise."

"French central heating?"

"Cognac, little one. The French swig it day and night from September to March. God! Paris in November! It doesn't fall below forty degrees, ever, but the damp in those pretty stone walls crawls into your marrow until you think nothing will ever get you warm again. In spite of their reputation for following the golden mean, the French are the drunkards of Europe. They don't get the credit for it because they don't get falling-down drunk like the English and the Germans; they get lit in the morning and nurse it along through the day until bedtime. It's their filthy climate, of course."

The blanket was pinned up, and it did intercept the thin draft from the window, as well as much of the light. Mona poured cognac and they drank.

"The French," she went on, "are the only civilized nation who ever had an absinthe problem. A good deal of nonsense has been circulated about absinthe containing drugs that rot the brain, and so forth. That's not true. Absinthe is simply commercially-pure alcohol, about 190 proof, doped up with anise and other flavors until it's drinkable. The beastly Arabs and Moroccans drank it as you'd expect, and then the civilized world encountered it. Nobody took to the muck except... of course... the French. It had to be outlawed as a narcotic... stupefiant in French, which God knows it was. It was smuggled in anyway, of course."

"Have you ever tasted it?"

"Of course. It's like cleaning fluid and licorice. I knew a painter in my salad days who was a true absinthe drinker. You mustn't ask me his name, but you'd know it. He'd wake in the morning and his little friend would hand him le premier...a tumbler full of the stuff. He'd sip it through breakfast and then be ready for the next, and so on. Disgusting."

"But interesting." And it was. The painter… was he Rouault, or Picabia or even Picasso? She smiled as Mona swayed, lily-like in the curtained dusk, to the little bar and poured again. She drank, wishing it were absinthe instead of brandy, something to link her more closely to the astonishing, brocaded world in which Mona moved gracefully.

"I haven't drunk this much since college," she said, and giggled. "Strange. I didn't like it then. It was just the thing to do. But I like it now."

"I'm so glad." The voice was a caress. "You seem to have… forgive me, little one… missed so much. But it's not too late. Clothes, travel, friendship with your own kind. And you're such a pretty little thing …"

Steady on, Mona told herself. She was coming close to stepping over the rules of the game. You never paid for it and you never made promises that you'd have to break. You didn't offer them riches, train tickets, fine raiment and lie as you did it. You, yourself alone, overpowered them without the leverage of their greed or you were no better than one of those dumpy, mannish creatures who slobbered over the pretty hostesses in the Paris clubs and paid them later for their tolerance and histrionics with many thousand-franc notes in some grubby hotel bedroom.

"…it saddens me a little to see your costume so… utilitarian."

Knowing exactly where she was heading, Joan Lundberg said a little breathlessly: "What do you suggest?"

Mona swept open her wardrobe trunk. "Help yourself, little one."

"I couldn't!"

"As a loan, then… just to try on."

"Very well." Her fingers moved among the dresses hanging from the rack on the right.

"No," Mona said lightly. "Not just to cover up. Glamour is from the skin out." She opened a drawer and stirred filmy underthings.

"I'm afraid it's too chilly for changing from the skin out."

"Alors, encore la chauffage centrale francaise!"

"My head's buzzing like a top now. Mona. Must I?"

"You must, little one. It's part of a sinister plan of mine. I'm going to get you helpless-drunk, pop you out the window where you'll quick-freeze in, say, twenty minutes and then live off you until spring when they come to rescue us. You didn't expect me to get along on a few miserable eggs and half a ham until April, did you?"

"Of course not, Mona," she said, giggling. "How could I be so disloyal. Turn the damper up on the French central heating." The stuff trickled down her throat and she fancied it radiated, glowing to her skin. She was not drunk, she told herself. She was having a wonderful, amusing time with a warm and wonderful woman whose touch was pleasant, with whom you could relax and feel pleasure that carried no terror of responsibility, no threat of shackling, unbreakable ties.

"I wore this yesterday," Mona was saying as she held up a lace and black satin corselet. "Our dimensions are about the same and it isn't a toothbrush after all …"

"It's lovely," Joan said decisively. She began to unbutton her wool dress. "Mona," she said, "I'll kill you if you say one word about my pants."

The snuggies emerged, sagging veterans of three Chicago winters. Mona Greer sputtered faintly. "Don't worry, darling. I'm a writer of sorts, but I couldn't begin to do them justice. It would take Edgar Allan Poe …"

Joan hurled them at her head and missed. "I warned you," she said. "Where is that thing? I'm freezing."

She stood in her stockings and shoes alone, dim in the room, feeling every hair-root of her body prickling into gooseflesh and her nipples strained and engorged in the cold air.

"Lovely," Mona Greer said absently, and held the corselet against her. Faintly it emitted her perfume. "Let me do the hooks, little one."

Behind her Mona Greer's deft hands worked, never quite touching her skin though she could feel their nearness and warmth, as the lace and satin folded about her in a firm embrace. A half-heard voice deep down in her cried: "You're hers now! Why did you do it?" and she shuddered, but now with the cold.

"Over in a moment, darling," Mona said, misunderstanding. The hands at last touched her thighs fleetingly as Mona Greer hooked the garters of the fabulous creation to her service-weight nylons in the rear. The contact was quite neutral when it occurred, but a moment later Joan had fiercely persuaded herself that it had been electrically thrilling. She hooked the garters in the front as Mona drew from the lingerie drawer of the trunk two ounces of black cobweb. Mona said carefully, holding the lace briefs up: "You'll notice that I'm not making any comparisons …"

Joan giggled and pulled them on. "How do I look?" she demanded.

"Like Ye Olde Tyme Courtesan."

"Swell," Joan said. "Give me a slip and a dress before I freeze."

The slip was white and extravagant with lace. Over it went a two-piece powder-blue wool suit dress that buttoned demurely at the wrists and neck.

"I suppose," Mona said studying her critically, "that it fits as well as an off-the-rack thing. And I like the thought of what's under that maidenly exterior; it tickles my lewd imagination."

"Mine too, though I never knew I had one until now."

"Darling, you've got lots of things …"

There were thudding feet outside and there was an angry medley of voices.

Joan opened the door; Mona Greer said sharply and a little too late: "Don't!"

Two kids in college-boy uniforms of sports coats and slacks were glowering at two other kids in army uniform. All four seemed to be good and drunk, and one of the college boys was saying fiercely: "You give me that goddam bottle back. You saw that fall off my seat."

"Din' see no such thing. Found it in the aisle. Finders keepers, losers weepers wheah we come from." The soldier had a brown pint bottle in his hand. He didn't take his eye off the college boy's half-cocked fists. "Nother gawdam word outta you an' A'll give you the bottle right in the face. Ah found it and Ah'm gonna keep it."

The other college boy tugged his friend's elbow. "Cut it out," he said. "That cracker means it. We'll tell the conductor later."

"Hi, baby," said the other soldier, seeing Joan in the door. He was drooling-drunk. "You wanna talk a li'l French to a fightin' man? Voolie-voo cooshay avec mwar? Swarsant-noof?"

Joan slammed the door and turned the bolt, raging. Mona Greer was laughing a silvery laugh. "Just a couple of redblooded American boys," she jeered. "Let's have a sloppy little lunch, darling. One egg or two?"

She took hard-boiled eggs from the paper bag under her berth and began to peel them.

"Two," said Joan distractedly, listening at the door. There was no more noise; the fight had aborted. "Brutes," she said.

"I can't think of a thing to say for them," Mona told her, as if confessing. "I'm a charitable person, but years of soul-searching leave me only more convinced that there isn't a man alive worth the powder to blow him to hell."

The words came unwillingly from Joan. She feared they would offend kind, warm Mona who had befriended her: "But you need them for children."

"And what do you need children for?" The riposte was swift and cutting as the sting of a wasp.

"I don't know," Joan said slowly. "I suppose it doesn't make a damn bit of difference whether the world keeps going or not. But I've always wanted children."

"Well, I can't give you one, darling, but I've always considered that an advantage. It's a hell of a world, little one, and I think the only solution to its problems is universal sterilization of men or women, it doesn't matter which, for one generation. Eat your eggs."

"Thanks." She nibbled at the tasteless things, suddenly found her appetite and finished them. "Did you really mean that, Mona?"

"Passionately." In the shadowed room, Mona Greer's eyes were caves of darkness. "It's all a farce, didn't you know?" She hauled herself up abruptly. Now what was she saying? What was spilling out unbidden? "It's this damned train," she said with a shiver. "It makes me think, and I don't like to."

"There was this girl I met, the Galapagos Islands girl. I didn't tell you, I didn't get around to it, but she was sure she'd die in childbirth and... she didn't seem to mind. She said she'd been sleeping around with a lot of the family field hands. She said they were nice guys."

"Diamonds in the rough," Mona Greer said tonelessly. "Like that specimen who just flattered you with the invitation in gutter-French."

Unreasonably Joan found herself defending the girl whose name she didn't even know, and by the defense attacking this woman who had been so good to her. "Maybe that soldier's all right. He was drunk and we don't know what he's been through or where he's going. Maybe I'd be just as dumb and crude back on his farm as he is on a train."

A chill went through Mona; a card-house seemed to be on the verge of collapse. "Trouble with you, Lundberg," she said lightly, "is you're not drinking. Shall I throw another log on the fire?"

"N-no, not just yet thanks, Mona. I wonder if they'll let me see her today."

Mona poured not a one-ounce pony but a three-ounce cocktail glass full of brandy and sipped it. "You can try," she said indifferently.

"I think I will." Joan got up, troubled. "I... I won't be long." She felt the satin embrace from her breasts to her thighs. "And I'll take good care of your lovely clothes, Mona."

"A bagatelle, little one. They're yours if you like."

Mona gulped the cognac and cursed herself after Joan left with a deprecating smile. She who would never pay for it was lowering herself to bribery, transgressing her own rules, the rules carefully laid out to prove that she was no slave of her senses but their mistress. It was this damned train, she thought greyly, lifting a corner of the blanket over the window. It was drifted deep with a billion dun crystals that matched her own leaden depression.

She tried to wrench her thoughts ahead to the final triumphant arrival in San Francisco, and how the story would add to her legend. Twittery Bozzy Hartman was a shrieking fag, but he knew everybody who counted in the bay city; he'd spread the word and magnify it. It would be good for a story in every paper, it would be good for sales of the damned book, and one had to think of that. One had to be a reasonable facsimile of a sculptor or writer or actress or businesswoman or even a wife. If you weren't Mona Greer the novelist you were pegged as Mona Greer the Lesbian, and that had to be kept in the background except at the right times and in the right places.

Maybe, she thought drearily, that's why so many of us practice the arts. It's an easy way to make a living or the world's best excuse for not making a living, depending on your talent and drive.

Lundberg was bucking her. It was the small independent income that was behind it; she was sure of that. When you have a few dollars coming in without having to work for them you're automatically freer and more dignified and sure than ordinary mortals.

If only Lundberg were one of the artsy-craftsy gals... Mona laughed silently, thinking of her second marriage and Mona Greer, Promoter of the Contemporary in American Crafts. Very handy indeed to have a little shop devoted to the finest in contemporary—not modern; somehow modern was a dirty word—leatherwear, ceramics, enamels and metalwork. They beat down her door—not customers, of course; nobody ever bought the damned ugly stuff—they beat down the door and begged her to put their junk on display, at any terms she wanted to make. And a Mona Greer could make interesting terms. It seemed during that wild and wonderful six months that at least one American girl in ten fancied that she was a handicrafter and that most of America's industrial plant was turning out pottery kilns, wheels, leather tools, blowtorches, solder, silversmithing stakes and hammers, glazes and clay for those girls. And then one morning she sighed as she realized that the inconspicuous fellow across the street had been there three days running, that he was in fact a plainclothesman, Vice Squad of course, and that it was time to shut up shop for good. You didn't want to get arrested. True enough and strange enough, there weren't any laws on the books anywhere making her little ways criminal per se; the gay boys were much worse off in that respect. It was a matter of definition, she supposed. You can't write a law against Lesbianism that doesn't also forbid one old gal to peck another on the cheek at a bridge party; one shaded into the other. But they could get you for loitering, for maintaining a disorderly house—that would be the charge they'd be building against her shop—or for spitting on the sidewalk if they were desperate and you were making a real public nuisance of yourself. But you didn't want to get arrested so you closed up the shop—anguished screams from the girls who thought they were female twentieth-century Cellinis—and went to California, just as you were doing now.

This damned train. That damned Lundberg bucking her. She'd pay for that, Mona thought, grinning crazily into the dark.

CHAPTER XXVIII

SNOW

"Conductor," Bill Loober said, "the trouble is people don't know what's coming next. Excuse me for saying so, but you're not letting them in on it. Now I think I can give them the facts if you'll just give them to me ..."

The conductor, driven beyond endurance, snarled: "Mister, the facts are that we're stuck, we're damn near out of food, we're damn near out of diesel oil and I don't know when the damn plows are going to get to us. Now keep your mouth shut about it."

Loober said gently: "Why, that's all right. That's all they want to know. I'm going to let them have the story, kid them along, get them to pool their blankets and any food they may have. It'll work out all right. You'll see."

But the conductor was gone, with a snort.

A simple matter of selling, Loober assured himself. The folks would go along as soon as they understood the situation... he walked from the diner to the first car. There was a screaming child, two squabbling women, several drunk men and scared tension on every face.

He stood on the end seat.

"Friends," he called out, "I've been talking to the conductor." That got attention; even the child stopped screaming and stared at him, open-mouthed. "It looks," Bill Loober said, "as though we're going to have to pull together to get through this thing with the least discomfort." Now sell them! "We don't just know right now when the plows will get here. Until they do, we've got to do the decent thing and share our possessions with our neighbors. Am I right, ma'am?"

His fingers shot at a weak-faced, middle-aged woman in black. She said: "Why, I suppose so ..."

"Of course!" he beamed. "That's the spirit! We're all okay in this car, I bet! Now, ma'am, have you got a spare blanket tucked away?"

"No," she said, suddenly shrill. "The maid says they're all gone ..."

His finger shot at a pudgy, blonde woman. "I see you have a spare." Damn right she did. She was sitting on three of the thin, grey blankets. "Folks, don't you think she ought to lend this lady a blanket?"

"Goddamn right!" yelled one of the drunks.

The blonde woman squawked: "I don't see why I should give up ..." But there was a growl from the people in the car, suddenly on the side of justice and fair play. Snarling, grudgingly, she handed one of the blankets to the woman, looking daggers at Loober.

"That's the spirit!" he yelled infectiously. "Give the lady a round of applause!" And he started off clapping, which the drunks took up, and then the rest of the car. The blonde woman actually was beaming at the end of it.

"Friends," Bill Loober orated, beaming, "let's get this organized. You, sir, would you please bring those blankets I see and put them here on the seat, and you, ma'am, will you please bring those blankets ..."

Meekly they did. He got them rationed out, two to a passenger, and had them liking it, proud of their good citizenship, shaking hands like a community sing...

And then the lights went out and the last thread of power-hum down the train from the locomotive stopped.

The women shrieked louder than he could bellow for everybody to be calm. Under his nose the blonde woman snatched back "her" blanket from the woman in black, who began to cry hopelessly. Two liquor-flushed men got into a fist-fight over a blanket that had been allotted to the child, who was shrieking again. Her father got into the fist-fight. The two drunks laid him out before returning to their own battle.

Bill Loober waded into the pandemonium and was caught by somebody's fist over his left ear.

"You ungrateful bastards!" he half-sobbed into the brawling dusk of the unlighted car. "You ought to be ashamed ..."

But nobody heard him, or if they did they paid no attention.

CHAPTER XXIX

"MRS." MACKENZIE

Joan's breath steamed lightly in the corridor. The passengers returning from the diner wore overcoats, sweaters, mufflers. It was more nervousness than cold, she told herself. It wasn't that cold... yet.

A woman was bickering impatiently with a tall trainman who looked sick. "What am I supposed to do, sit and count my fingers until your precious snowplows get here? I want to read and I want some light to read by. I never heard of such a thing ..."

Between the two of them they blocked the passage. A rearbound man fidgeted through the harangue and finally said in a clear, poisonous voice: "Get out of the way, sister. I got to go to the can."

She gaped and stepped aside and started all over again, demanding that the trainman do something about the insult. He listened without a word, looking sick, until she ran down, said tonelessly: "Yes ma'am," and went away.

The woman turned to Joan and spouted: "Did you ever hear of such insolence? We should get up a letter to the company ..."

"Excuse me," Joan said, and pushed past, hurrying until she made it to the next car. Foreman was lounging by the green curtains of the men's room. He nodded curtly as if he didn't want to talk. She gave him a meager smile and went on to the fat girl's compartment with a weird sensation that the train was tilted downhill, that she was falling all the way and that it leveled off only at the compartment door.

She wasn't, by God, going to be turned away this time. She'd think of something...

It was the doctor who opened the door and not his testy little wife. "Hello," he said. "What can I do for you?"

"I thought there might be something I could do for you," she said firmly. "I've had some nurse's training. Maybe I can relieve you for a while."

"Good," he said distractedly. "I have to go down the hall and my wife's out like a light. I didn't want to wake her. Come in."

She did. "Hi," the fat girl said from her berth. Her face was like clay. "I'm between pains."

"This lady's going to watch you for a couple of minutes," the doctor said. To Joan he whispered: "No need to touch her. If there's a syncope or the pulse becomes much weaker come and get me. I'll rush anyway." He threw a confident smile at the fat girl and left them.

Joan sat by the girl and took her pulse… regular, fast and weak. "I don't even know your name," she said to the girl, "but I've been thinking about you."

"It's a killer. Pilar Mackenzie y del Torres. Spanish mother. But names you can do something about. They call me Mack."

"Okay, Mack. I'm Joan Lundberg. Swedish father. They call me Joan. What's going on down there?"

"I got a big pain that's the start of second-stage labor, he thinks. He can't do a live Caesarian: no proper anaesthetics or instruments. My guess is he's waiting for me to kick off and then he'll do it posthumous."

"Oh, Mack!" Joan said, agonized.

There was one rap on the door and Foreman walked in.

"What are you doing here?" Joan asked sharply.

"Came to see if the lady needed anything. I lent her my coat and it occurred to me that she might need some hot water like in the movies or something like that …" his eyes were darting around the little cubicle.

"Oh," Mack said amiably, "you're the fellow. Thanks …" A spasm went across her clay-colored face. "Hang on," she said. "Here we go again. Make a note of the time …" Her fingers clawed at Joan's arm as the contraction shuddered through her, and her lips writhed away from her teeth. Under Joan's middle finger her pulse fluttered and pounded, stronger, not weaker. She didn't yell. It seemed to go on for an hour. The second hand on Joan's wrist watch crawled like a minute hand on a clock around the dial once before her blurred eyes, twice, and half around again before the girl relaxed with a shuddering sigh. "That was a big one," she whispered. "You're supposed to feel the head crown, but I didn't that time."

"I'm sure it'll be soon," Joan said. "I'm sure it'll be all right, Mack. You mustn't think it won't. You'll be all right." She was aware through the back of her head that Foreman was no longer in the cubicle and wondered dimly why he had come, what he had done and why he had gone.

The doctor came in without knocking, looking greatly relieved, and said: "Thank you," to Joan. He took the girl's wrist from her fingers and said after a moment: "You're surprising me, Mrs. Mackenzie. That's all right."

"There was another pain, doctor."

"We'll have a look." He turned to the compact dressing table, his open bag and an enamel pan full of blue liquid on its top, and rinsed his hands. Joan saw on the table, behind the bag where they could not be seen from the berth, an array of glittering scalpels and retractors. They were not lying in a pan of bichloride of mercury. The flesh they were ready to shear through would be forever beyond the danger of infection.

"I've got to go now," Joan said, choking on the words.

"'bye," the girl said weakly. "Doctor, can she come back and see me later?"

"I suppose …" the doctor began, and broke off, looking curiously into his black bag, letting the blue fluid drip into the pan. He dismissed the thought, whatever it was, and said: "I suppose so, later. Thanks very much, Miss…?"

"Lundberg. Doctor, if you need me or if there's anything I can do I'm in Compartment C, Car 17. If you can't remember ask the porter for Miss Greer's compartment."

His face fell into disapproval. "I see," he said. "Thank you for the offer, Miss Lundberg."

She went out, her face flaming. He saw. What did he see? She had done nothing! Who the hell did he think he was to pass judgment on her and Mona? Sanctimoniously he had called Mack "Mrs." though he must have seen there was no ring. If fornication was all right with him what was wrong with… she couldn't bring herself to express the word. Anyway, she had done nothing. She had only made friends with a remarkable woman who had a great deal to offer intellectually.

She stalked down the aisle, back to Mona's compartment, her steps growing slower and slower. Abreast of the door she stopped…and then went on, slowly, to the next car, upper and lower berths only, where she belonged. She could see Boyce in his half of their shared seat.

Joan ducked blindly into the green-curtained ladies' room and dropped into the leather seat. The leather was cold, and she felt the embrace of lace and satin tighten around her like an Iron Maiden. Her breath steamed into the cold air and she wanted her good cloth coat desperately but could not bring herself to rise and get it from the dim compartment she shared with her fascinating new friend.

A woman on the seat whom she had not even noticed, a woman bundled in a leopard coat… no, it was stenciled rabbit of course… said to her sympathetically: "Don't let it get you down. The plows'll be here in two hours."

"How do you know?" Joan asked hopelessly.

"My husband found out from the conductor."

"How does the conductor know?"

The woman stared at her. "Well, it's his business. I guess he knows his business."

"I hope so."

"You're a cheerful one, aren't you?" the woman marveled.

Suddenly there was complete silence. The last residual hum transmitted along the cars from the locomotive far ahead stopped, and simultaneously the dimly-glowing light bulbs went out. And stayed out.

"My God!" the woman said, in an appalled whisper. She got up and hurried out.

To her husband, Joan thought dully.

* * * *

Boyce had fallen into a light doze. When the power went off he woke with a start and blinked at the uneven light filtering through the snow-crusted windows into the car. A woman chattered hysterically behind him and a man was trying to calm her down.

"What happened?" he asked, turning.

"Your guess is as good as mine, brother," the man said. The woman shut up with a stranger's eyes on her and looked embarrassed. "The lights went out and the engine stopped. I guess it froze up or something... they don't build them to perform as stationary power plants."

"I guess that means the heat goes too?"

"I guess so. The heat must have been electric, maybe plus heat from the diesels. Either way, it's off. I wish to hell we could start a fire ..."

"Why not? There must be some kind of circulation for the air."

"Harvey, don't be crazy," the woman said, patting her hair. She explained to Boyce, very lady-like: "A Mr. Fixit from way back."

"You keep out of it, dear. At least we can try." He lit a cigarette and blew a plume of smoke at the roof of the car. "See?" he said. "It goes into those slot things. I bet it would work."

The tall, harried trainman rushed past.

"Conductor!" Harvey miscalled him sharply.

He stopped like a gaffed fish and turned slowly. "Yes, mister?"

"I was wondering if we could build a fire. The cigarette smoke seems to go out through those slot things ..."

"A fire? Hell, no, mister! You can't do that. You just keep calm; I'm going up to see what the word is from the engineer. We'll prob'ly have power on again soon." He rushed ahead.

"What about a fire?" asked a middle-aged woman across the aisle. "I surely could use one, but is it safe?"

"Sure," said Harvey. His wife rolled her eyes to heaven as he explained about the cigarette smoke and the woman nodded understandingly as the audience grew.

"Let's try it with a newspaper," somebody said.

A twisted page of the Chicago Tribune was ignited. Harvey waved it like a torch, explaining: "See? It goes into those slot things ..." and broke off with a hacking cough as he got a lungful of smoke and dropped the blazing paper to the carpeted aisle. It was stamped out and Harvey explained that it was just a tricky draft, but it didn't go down. He sat sulkily beside his wife, passengers drifted back to their seats and Boyce sat slumped, listening to the sporadic bickering behind him as the darkness and the coldness grew.

* * * *

Foreman was among the last at luncheon. The ten one-grain tablets of morphine sulfate from the vial in the doctor's black bag were burning a hole in his pocket, but he deliberately forced himself to turn left instead of right as he slipped out of the one-woman maternity ward and headed for the diner. Let her wait, he thought listlessly. He didn't owe her a thing, nor did she owe him. He would give her the tablets as a minor courtesy; just as she had lent him her body. It hadn't meant anything in particular to either of them, except that it was better than sitting and waiting. Intensity had gone out of both their lives. She was a puppet of the one-grain tablets, he was a puppet of the red-faced businessmen. They had no big decisions left before them; things would just keep happening unavoidably. She would continue to take off until her foot slipped and she landed in the gutter. He would continue to do Syndicate chores until his foot slipped and he landed in the Drainage Canal with crabs on his face. No decisions any more: just mild choices. Bacon or sausage for breakfast. Salad or soup for lunch. Roast beef or pork chops for dinner. This tart or that for the night.

He thought mildly of living with her during his weeks in San Francisco. He'd be doing a highly technical, absorbing, exacting job all day. It might be good to relax at night by committing adultery, putting the horns on an absent professional soldier who was guarding him while he slept. Her husband would be overseas in a few days and it would be a really rotten thing to do and so quite in keeping with him. The woman wasn't as good as she thought she was, but she was pretty good.

He got a table to himself. Lines were drawn through most of the things on the luncheon card. He checked the Vienna Cutlet with Poached Egg and the waiter apologetically told him that it would have to be an eggless cutlet today; seemed like all the eggs were just gone.

"They're handy little things to have around, aren't they?" he asked the waiter blandly.

"Suh?"

"Skip it. I'll take the cutlet." Waiting, he thought of Joan Lundberg who still had a decision before her—exactly one decision. Straight or queer. She was a whole-hearted girl; he knew the type. If she went for politics, she got in up to her neck. If she went for Mona's brand of fun she wouldn't be one of the dabblers, one of the ambiguous people who take it or leave it alone, depending on circumstances. She was a woman who had to justify herself and be sure she was right, prove she believed in a way of life by living it to the hilt. One decision left. The wrong way, it led into a shabby, clandestine world of perverts and blackmail. God damn Mona Greer to hell, and what was holding up his cutlet?

* * * *

His compartment door was latched from the inside. He knocked and announced: "Landlord for the rent money, lady." The lieutenant's wife opened the door carefully, not letting herself be seen.

"Have you got them?"

"Here they are," he said, counting them into her palm. "You don't mind a few tobacco crumbs, do you?"

"Ha ha," she said. She stared at the pills for a long moment and then put them in her handbag.

"There's something I don't get," he said. "No needle marks on you. What do you do with it if you don't inject it with a hypodermic?"

"Of course you don't get it, lover boy." She spoke with condescending bravado, the air of a known defiant homosexual, a prison lifer—or an admitted addict. "You've been going to too many movies. I love Frank Sinatra with all my heart and soul, but his idea of an addict would make a cat laugh. Needles are for saps. They leave marks, as you wisely observed, and sometimes they leave abscesses that send you to the hospital, and sometimes they give you blood poisoning and you lose an arm or a leg. It all goes to the same place," she said condescendingly. "If you swallow the stuff you get a slow glow that lasts. If you sniff it it gets to the brain faster and you get a brighter glow that doesn't last. If you inject it, you get what a fellow told me was a 'ping'. Now, do I look stupid enough to invite an abscessed leg for a lousy ping?"

"I see," he said with a straight face. "You know exactly what you're doing."

She looked up at him suspiciously and changed the subject. "What took you so long, anyway?" she snapped.

"I had to wait for the doctor to go down the hall. Just be glad his bag wasn't locked."

"I am, lover boy. How's the girl with the baby?"

"Dying."

"Tough," she said flatly. "I think she spotted me for a user on sight. So did the doctor and so did you. Does it stick out all over me?"

"Hell, no. Don't worry about it. You must be wrong about the fat girl. How could she possibly? The doctor, hell, that's to be expected. And me, I've seen hundreds in the lineups and still it was just a wild guess."

"Thanks," she said with a wintry smile. "I'm going to go and find the lieutenant." She kissed him expertly.

"Thanks," he said back. He opened the door and looked up and down the corridor. "Okay."

She slid out gracefully.

"Hollow," he said, thinking of her. "Like a dead tree with a few green shoots still to die." Let Joan Lundberg be turned into that?

The thin vibration of the train went dead and the lights went out. "God-damn it," he said. Joan Lundberg would be in Greer's arms tonight.

But not if he could help it.

He got up and went out.

CHAPTER XXX

SNOW

The old conductor was sitting in the galley of the club car with his head in his hands. The tall trainman found him there at last, after searching everywhere.

"Mr. Nichols," he said.

"Oh, go away, kid," the conductor groaned.

"I got to ask you something. The toilets are freezing. What'll we do?"

The conductor sat up wearily. "Unlock a couple of the car doors. Women on the right and men on the left."

"Is that safe, Mr. Nichols? That soldier got frostbit."

"The passengers have got to use their heads sometime. It might as well be now. A few seconds outside won't kill 'em. And it'll be better than stinking up the train. Then people start heaving. Pass the word to the crew. Lock the toilets when you get a chance."

"Okay, Mr. Nichols," the tall trainman said.

The conductor sagged in the chair again, his head in his hands.

CHAPTER XXXI

SWITCH-BLADE

Mona Greer heard the knock on her compartment door and composed herself a little more sleekly on the berth. The blonde had taken her time. She would pay for that. "Come in, little one," she called in a silvery voice. "It's not locked."

It wasn't Joan Lundberg standing in the door. It was Foreman, the wire service toughie. He had no overcoat on and his tie was askew. He seemed to be just a little drunk. "I know that invitation wasn't for me," he said, "but I took advantage of it anyway."

Mona smiled. He was angry, but everything would be all right. The faint note of apology and uncertainty in his voice, all the more marked because he was trying to repress it, told her that. He was one down; he was just a wire service toughie with problems. She was one up; she was the famous Mona Greer, whose Thighs of the Wild Mare had surfboated on the Herald Tribune list of ten fiction best-sellers for eight weeks in the spring and was still skimming nicely along. And both of them knew it.

"Sit down," she said. "Would you like a blanket to drape around you?"

"Thanks," he said, and took one of the neatly-folded spares from the dressing table. He put it on like a shawl, gratefully, and Mona almost laughed aloud. What a fool! To let himself be costumed grotesquely in a thin gray blanket before quarreling with a woman sleek in mink!

"A drink?" she asked, rising gracefully.

"Rye?"

"Surely." She poured. "It was good of you to ease my loneliness, Mr. Foreman. How are things outside? I've pulled my hole in after me."

"Not good, not bad. Everybody's scared and scared of showing it. A few hysterical women and children, but no general panic. I guess that's because we're laid out in a long string and you can't have a panic that way. We're a long string of little groups. If one group gets frantic it thins out in each direction... where's Joan?"

"I really don't know. She seems to have deserted me. She was going to see that woman in labor, but I'm sure they wouldn't let her stay with her this long."

"I know. She was with her for a few minutes." He drank and said: "Maybe she's with Boyce."

Mona Greer smiled. "That's entirely up to her, don't you think?"

"You know damned good and well it isn't. Why don't you lay off the kid?"

She knew it was put more crudely than he had meant to, and sooner. Now she could pretend not to understand. Foreman could become specific, she could become outraged and he'd have to admit he had no proof and back out, confused. That was one way, and there would be a certain amount of kick in it. There were other ways, possibly with more kick in them.

"I suppose," she said, "this is what you'd call 'talking turkey'!" In her mouth the words were gross and sardonic. "Yes," he said doggedly. He pulled the absurd shawl around him.

"Why don't you like me?" she asked quietly. "Why don't people let us alone?" Her grin was inward. Foreman was a self-doubter; now let him doubt his motives and the justice of his meddling.

"Don't get me wrong," he said after a pause. "I'm not a fairy-slugger. Other things being equal, I've hired them to work for my firm and I've met them socially. What I don't like is wolves. Not any more than I like rapists or bank-robbers or muggers or pickpockets."

"When you've been hurt," Mona said slowly, "all you want is for the pain to stop. We have been hurt. We didn't ask to be what we are. If Miss Lundberg wants to be my friend isn't that her affair? Must you say to her; no, anything but that. Go to a psychiatrist, or lock yourself in a cell, or deny your instincts and be satisfied with second-best or with nothing." Which, she thought, turned the argument neatly upside-down. The expression of delicate pain did not leave her face.

"Look," said Foreman. "I don't know how to put it to you, but you seem to be an honest person even if you're on the wrong side of the fence."

How wrong you are, toughie. How amusingly wrong you are.

"She's got a chance with Boyce," he said. "They go together. I don't want to get this mixed up with Hollywood bunk, but they ring bells in each other. And then you stepped in. Can't you just step out again? What's it to you, anyway?"

"Mr. Foreman, when you see a crying child don't you want to comfort her?" Mona demanded. Her voice was agitated; she strode the little length of the compartment and lit a cigarette, snapping her gold lighter hard. "I saw Joan lost and crying in a world she doesn't understand, denying her instincts because she's been taught to, told that her instincts are filthy and abnormal. She looked at me and saw what she wanted, what she's been wanting for years: a special love, a special tenderness. Do you want me to slam the door on her and say: it's not for you? You want it but you can't have it. Mr. Foreman disapproves. In his opinion you'd be better off stealing Mr. Boyce from his wife, and his opinion is more important than what you feel in your bones."

Foreman clutched the blanket impotently; his breath was a white cloud in the compartment.

There was a deferential rap on the door.

"Come in," Mona called, composedly.

It was the porter. He had a screaming plaid overcoat on top of his white, round-collared jacket. "Excuse me, ma'am," he said. "I don't know whether you noticed about the toilet yet ..."

"What is it?"

"They're freezing and the pullman conductor said to say he thinks nobody better use them, be better to go outside." He smiled deprecatingly. "He's gonna put the steps out and unlock the train doors. He says maybe it be better if ladies go out on the right and gennulmen on the left. Can you remember that, ma'am? Ladies on the right and gennulmen on the left... and be better not to get far from the train."

"All right," Mona Greer said wearily. "Thank you."

When he left she flipped up the lid of the commode, ignoring Foreman, and tried the handle. The little trap didn't work and no water came to flush the bowl.

"Well, Mr. Foreman," she said, without turning around, "have you said your piece?"

"Yes," he said.

"Very well." She turned, grinning, and saw his face whiten. "My advice to you, young man, is to take it outside on the left where the gennulmen go and deposit it gently on the snow where it belongs. You're talking to the wrong girl. Now listen to the facts of my life: I know what I want and I take it. What I want tonight is that little blonde twist and I'm going to have her, make no mistake about that. If you think you can stop me, you're welcome to try. But I wouldn't bet a nickel on your chances. This has been very amusing, but I'm little tired now....you'll forgive me for saying that you are a somewhat tiresome young man. I'll be delighted to see you for cocktails at six. Miss Lundberg will be here; I guarantee that."

She read his face as she spoke, gloatingly drinking his pain and frustration and hate. He raged as she offered the casual invitation, which meant that he didn't matter: he could come or not come, try or not try as he pleased. If he didn't no loss. If he did, she could watch him squirm on the pin.

But last came an expression which she couldn't read and which gave her no pleasure: a cool blankness. He said tonelessly: "Thank you for making it so clear. I'd be delighted to come for cocktails. May I take the blanket with me? You seem to have blankets to spare."

"Please do," she said graciously. He left, stiff-backed and clutching the absurd shawl around him. Though she did not notice it, his knuckles were white. When the door closed behind him Mona laughed with delight over the episode; it had been a perfect thing of its kind. Except, she thought, suddenly puzzled, for his odd coldness at the last. He suddenly had ceased to feel pain or shame or anger. It was odd…

Walking blindly, icily through the train, Foreman knew an idea was surfacing, no matter how hard he might try to keep it down. It was one of the big things, like a million dollars or an auto crash or being elected to the Senate or losing one's virginity. Maybe half a dozen big things happen to a person in a lifetime and Foreman felt that his was about to be enriched by one. What he proposed to himself was that he murder Mona Greer.

It was a very big thing, he discovered as he examined it. The murder of Mona Greer would not be at all like most murders. Most murders, detective novels to the contrary notwithstanding, are silly, simple, drunken head-bashings, usually of a spouse's head following a quarrel about money or sex. To the poor fools who did these things in their fury Foreman now felt condescending; his job was much more difficult, and was complicated by the fact that he didn't want to be caught and electrocuted.

He thought too of the gang murders. His home, Chicago, was an unusually good place to study them. There have been, he thought, about seven hundred of these killings in the past twenty-five years in Chicago; he rather doubted that as many as ten of the killers had been convicted. And Chicago's miserable rate of conviction was said to be better than that of twenty other American cities.

Was there a lesson for him there in how to murder Mona Greer? Probably not. The gang killers were professionals, invariably imported just before the job and immediately exported after it. They were unbelievably crude and casual about their killing; all they asked was reasonable, not absolute, privacy and a finger man. When the victim was pointed out to them they shot him full of holes and went away. What did a few identifications matter? They were many states away from the scene, there were alibi witnesses galore for them, and if some maniac insisted on his identification of the killers, why, there were ways of handling that too.

It wasn't for him. He didn't have the organization going for him. It was queer that he belonged to such an organization, that he had spoken a couple of days ago with men who had ordered such killings, but he could not avail himself of their resources. They wouldn't even understand why it had to be done. Killings were for business, were to keep the boys in line, were not for personal—or altruistic, God forbid!—reasons.

His painfully acquired military experience was turning out to be no help at all. What he proposed was a very different thing from lying on one's belly on a forward slope, squinting through binoculars at distant puffs of white smoke and muttering into a soundpower phone: "One zero zero left... five zero right... fire for effect, fire for effect ..." Such squinting and muttering had resulted in perhaps thirty deaths, including the spectacular obliteration of a truck that must have been loaded with land mines, and he was learning that it had nothing to do with civil murder.

Walking icily, blindly through the train, Foreman told himself: Kill her. You've sunk for the third time and so has the junkie red-head. Kill Greer and let Joan and Boyce be free to work out their happiness or bungle it. You can't hand them a story-book or Hollywood perfect romance, but you can give them their freedom to try and make one. If they fail it'll be honest failure, not a pratt-fall into a filthy gutter, tripped up by the daintily-shod, carelessly-extended foot of Mona Greer.

"Watch it, pappy," somebody said, lurching past him in the narrow aisle. One of the college boys was lurching into one of the green-curtained smoking rooms, and an immediate bellow sounded from behind the curtains.

"For God's sake, kid, didn't you hear what the conductor said? You want to stink out the whole train?"

"Listen, mister," the boy's voice yelled, "You can go to hell. You can also—"

There was a sharp click and Foreman looked between the curtains. The young man was lying on the floor with his pants down, rubbing his jaw wonderingly. A red-faced man was standing over him feeling his right fist painfully.

From the floor the kid said in a low, poisonous voice: "Now, you bastard, I'm going to cut your goddam ..." His hand snaked into his pocket and came out with a blue plastic handle. Snick. It was three inches of gleaming steel...

Foreman unhesitatingly stepped in with his left foot and swung the right hard against the young man's head. His heel connected with the temple and the kid went down with a groan, the switch-blade tinkling from his hand. He stayed down, his face the color of veal.

The red-faced man kicked the knife a yard away from the limp body and picked it up with his left hand, carrying the right crossed against his chest. He was sweating marbles from his forehead. "Thanks, mister," he said to Foreman, panting. "I think I broke my hand on his thick skull ..."

There were awed faces looking through the green curtain. "Somebody get that doctor," the red-faced man said sharply to them. "This boy fell and hurt himself. Didn't he?"

"Sure," said one of the faces. "I'll get the doctor."

The man sat down dizzily and tucked his hand into his coat like Napoleon. He got up again at once and said to Foreman: "Let's get out of here, friend." Two or three men were kneeling over the limp figure of the young man, muttering and probing clumsily.

"He's okay," one of them said. "I can feel his heart."

Foreman and the man with the broken hand slid out. "I wonder if he would've cut me," the man said, and then realized that to wonder this was less than gratitude. "Sure," he answered himself. "I guess you saved my life or something like that. Anything I have is yours, unto the half of my kingdom and my daughter's hand. On second thought, her husband might not like that. Will you settle for a drink and a couple of sandwiches? I made a little deal with the diner steward. If pressed-ham sandwiches were money I'd be Jock Whitney."

"Okay," Foreman said. "You want the doctor to have a look at that hand?"

"I don't want anything to do with it," the man said emphatically.

"Publicity-shy?"

"You could say that, friend. The wife didn't even know I was in Chicago. This is my place."

It was a drawing room. Foreman made a sling out of a hand-towel and tied it behind the man's neck, and got the sandwiches from a suitcase and the liquor from under the berth. The man drank almost a tumblerful in two big gulps and shuddered.

"That's better," he said. "God knows how I'm going to explain this. I was supposed to be in Washington, I guess they'll publish the passenger lists. I was afraid you fractured that guy's skull in there, friend."

"He'll be all right," Foreman said. "Or not. What the hell does it matter?"

The man looked at him closely for a moment and said: "Have a drink. It'll keep the cold out." He flourished the bottle, a surprisingly cheap blended rye to find in a drawing room. "It's good stuff," he said. "I'm on the distribution end."

Foreman looked at the label… Old Somethingorother. Well, he knew about Old Somethingorother. They made it in Peoria, in the same stills that had run through Prohibition, financed by the same gangster money, distributed by the same respectable dummies.

He took a drink of the stuff; it went down, as always, like a machinist's coarse half-round file.

"I can't use your daughter, friend," he said to the red-faced man, "but could I have that knife?"

"Hell, yes," the man said, scrabbling for it with his left hand in his pocket. "Just don't tell anybody where you got it."

He handed it over with relief.

Foreman let it lie in his palm and tentatively pressed the button. Snick. Three inches of gleaming steel. He folded it into the handle, put it carefully in his pocket and said: "Thanks."

He walked out into the corridor and to his own compartment.

* * * *

The Reverend Mr. Groves, who was a doctor but not a Reverend Doctor, having only a B.D. to go with his B.Sc. and M.D., looked down at the girl and thought: "I'll have to intervene." The baby would not crown, the cervix would not dilate sufficiently, she was obese and her heart was in its last extremities.

"Ergotrate," he said to his wife, his nurse.

She shook a small pill from one of the tubes in his bag and placed it far back on Mrs. Mackenzie's dry tongue. The girl choked and swallowed as she poured water after the pill.

"When you feel the next one, Mrs. Mackenzie," said the doctor, "bear down. Bear down for all you're worth."

The futile contractions were only exhausting her.

She looked at him blankly. She was sweating in spite of the cold; her skin was dead-looking and tallowy. She mumbled something: "Mamacita."

Delirium on top of everything else; she would be unable to cooperate with what little strength she had left. The chance of her survival dropped from a hundred to one on down to a thousand.

"Can you hear me, Mrs. Mackenzie? Say yes if you can hear me."

"Bless me father for I have sinned," she murmured.

The ergotrate hit and there was a huge contraction; her bulging stomach sucked in as if she had been kicked. Dr. Groves saw the infant's crown and reached for it with his hands, trying to get a purchase on the slippery wet skin. As he struggled for a hold the girl croaked again, insistently: "Bless me father for I have sinned. Bless me father for I have sinned. Why don't you answer me father."

"She thinks you're a priest," said the nurse.

The contraction subsided and the baby was still unborn; he had not been able to get the hold. "O.B. forceps," he said to his wife. And to the girl: "Are you truly penitent?" His wife, reaching for the two loose halves of the forceps paused to give him an incredulous look.

She muttered: "Yes father truly penitent."

Groves took the forceps and waited for another contraction when he might have a chance to use them. He inserted one half; the next thing to do was insert the other and lock them together. That he could not do until another contraction; there was simply no room. He could have hammered the second half home, perhaps, but it would have killed mother and child. "Father," said the girl. He felt her pulse and thought back to the Comparative Religion courses in the seminary.

"When did you make your last confession?" he asked.

She said: "Many years ago father. Since then I have sinned. I committed adultery. Once. I am truly penitent."

His hand on her pulse, he said: "I absolve you in the name of the Father and of the Son and of the Holy Ghost." His wife dropped a haemostat. He went on: "You will say one Our Father as penance." Her lips began to move. After a while they stopped moving. She whispered: "You'll be sure the baby's baptized, father. Very important."

"I'll see to it," he said, and then felt her pulse stop altogether. He waited thirty seconds by his wristwatch and said: "She's gone. Scalpel."

He carved recklessly through layer after layer of tissue; they delivered the baby within seconds. It was dark and still in his hands. "Contrast plunges," he snapped to his wife, and began to blow gently into the baby's mouth. She ran from the compartment to the galley in the diner behind their car; she returned within minutes followed by two cooks, one with a dishpan of hot water and one with cold. One of the cooks said: "Fore God, it's a little black child."

Mrs. Groves looked and saw he was correct; she simply hadn't noticed before that the child was coffee-colored. "Thank you, gentlemen," she said. "That will be all."

Groves continued the artificial respiration as he dipped the infant alternately in the hot and cold water. Now and then a pulse flickered in the small body and once or twice the baby seemed on the point of drawing a full breath, but never made good on the promise. After thirty minutes Groves put the body down. "No use," he said to his wife.

"Can't save 'em all."

Groves took in his palm a little of the water from one of the pans and dropped it on the brow of the infant. "Ego te baptizo," he murmured, "in nomine Patris et Filii et Spiritu Sancti." Looking sidelong at his wife he added: "I did tell her I would. Well, let's close up Mrs. Mackenzie. Sutures, please."

CHAPTER XXXII
LADIES AND GENTLEMEN

Joan Lundberg sat in a half-trance in the bitter cold of the ladies' room as the afternoon light filtering darkly through the drifted windows dimmed. Five minutes more, she told herself dazedly, and then I'll go to Mona's compartment for my coat. And then five minutes more. And then five minutes more.

The pullman maid put her head in to announce about the toilets... ladies on the right and genmun on the left. A woman cackled that she never heard of such a thing and that she wouldn't dream of it. Another woman asked testily whether she thought she was Queen Victoria.

Joan sat through it dazedly.

A kind lady finally asked her if she didn't have a coat.

"Yes," Joan said, "I have a coat," and the woman went away.

The cackling woman came back at last, furtively, and ducked into one of the booths, very lady-like.

The place became intolerable and Joan got up and went to Mona's compartment and knocked.

Mona Greer opened the door, tall and sleek in her dark mink. There were no reproaches or questions; just a warm acceptance of her return. "How was the girl, little one?" Mona asked.

"Girl?"

"The one with the baby."

"Oh. I saw her for a couple of minutes. She's having a hard time. A terribly hard time." Wildly: "What the hell did she expect?"

Mona laughed warmly. "You're learning," she said approvingly.

"Give me a drink, please. I'm freezing." She found her coat and belted it around her, breathing steam into the air. The cognac burned her throat gratifyingly.

"Mr. Foreman popped in for a few minutes," Mona said carefully, "to lecture me on my evil ways. But he'll be back like a lamb soon for cocktails. Getting dark, isn't it? Soon there won't be anything to do except go to bed."

"I don't mind. Mona, must we have those men in? It would be ridiculous. Charging around in the dark, spilling drinks ..."

"It should be amusing, darling. We won't be ridiculous." Joan laughed a little hysterically. She was right of course; as always, she was right. It would be amusing, and there was damn-all in life except amusement, at least life as Mona Greer lived it.

Boyce felt a call of nature and thought: Oh, damn! He got up from the warmish nest he had made in the seat with a blanket and his overcoat and stumped down the aisle. Women on the right, men on the left. The stench from the green-curtained men's room was sickening. Somebody had not been cooperative. He was very glad he didn't have a seat near the vestibule.

He opened the train door and clinging cautiously to the grabirons, went down the three steps of the wooden box-ladder planted in the snow. The cold grabbed him and squeezed his chest: a dry, ringing cold that you didn't notice for a second and then noticed all too well.

This was the drifted-in side of the train. With shovels somebody had scooped a kind of cave, open to the leaden sky. The other side of the train the snow wouldn't be more than a foot or so deep... good break for the ladies. But that of course was why they'd done it that way. He was glad there was nobody else out. Hastily he relieved himself, arranged his clothes and scurried up the steps. He had forgotten to put his gloves back on and the grabirons burned his palms.

Shame-faced, he scurried down the aisle to his seat, and found it occupied by two fattish, determined, scowling women. "That's my seat," he said politely. "See? There's my baggage ..."

"We were wondering," one of the women said, "if you'd be so kind as to change places with us. We're in three and five, and the... odor ..."

He stood bewildered.

A woman across the aisle leaned over and said: "Don't do it, mister. Queen Victoria there is the one that made the odor, all by herself. I saw her sneak in after I tried to talk sense to her. She's a lady, she is."

"Oh, what a lie!" the woman by the window whooped. "How dare you ..." And then she began to cry and said: "Come on, Milly." Drably they trailed back to seats by the ladies' room.

Boyce said to the woman: "Well, thanks," and began to settle himself. And then got thirsty. He went down the aisle to the little fountain and of course it didn't work.

A man passing stopped and watched him contemptuously for a moment as he pressed the handle and then tried to twist it. "It's frozen, Jack," he said. "If you want water you go out, gets some snow and thaw it with your hands. That's all I been doing for two hours for my little girl. I don't know where she puts it."

"Thanks," Boyce said. The hell with the water anyway. It was getting darker. Soon he'd be able to cash in on the invitation to cocktails. He didn't want the liquor especially. He did want very much to see Joan even in his role of a bumbling male showed up and made ridiculous by Mona Greer, damn her.

* * * *

Foreman sat in the half-dark of his compartment with the blanket huddled around him. There was a rap on his door.

"Come in."

It was Groves, the doctor-preacher. He had Foreman's storm coat over his arm. "I want to thank you," he said hesitantly.

"Oh. What happened?"

"She died, Mr. Foreman. In a state of grace, I hope. Do you mind if I sit down for a moment?" He slumped onto the other end of the berth and dropped the coat between them.

"I'm sorry," Foreman said inadequately. "What about the baby?"

"It was touch-and-go for half an hour. And then he died. About a month premature. In a hospital I'd have popped him into an incubator but—" He fell wearily silent.

Foreman had to know. "I heard," he said, "that a young man got hurt." He licked his lips.

The doctor looked at him dryly. "My wife first-aided him. I'm sure you'll be glad to hear that he's resting well and that he suffered no fractures when he fell and hit his head. I gather it was his own carelessness that caused him to fall and hit his head."

"Yes," said Foreman, relieved. He held up the coat to what light filtered through the window. It was clean. He slipped it on gratefully and buttoned and buckled it from chin to the hem.

"Mr. Foreman," Groves said, stirring with an effort from his fatigue.

"Yes, doctor?"

"I don't think you should say anything to anybody about Mrs. Mackenzie and the baby. There would be no point spreading alarm and despondency."

"I won't. You don't have to go, doctor. You seem to be dog-tired." Groves was getting up.

"Yes I do have to go. Silly woman went out in baby-doll pumps—so my wife tells me they're called—and dawdled over her business. Three frostbitten toes on one foot, two on the other. Her brilliant husband rubbed them with snow. Naturally blood-vessels were ruptured. If she's lucky there will be no gangrene. Of course she was a diabetic, too, and should have known better …"

The doctor wandered from the compartment, passing his hand wearily over his face.

A good man, thought Foreman, who couldn't set things right because of an accident of wind and weather. How could he in his corruption set a thing right? He felt the switch-blade knife in his pocket, hard and cold as his hate.

CHAPTER XXXIII

NIGHTFALL

Newscast:

"The thoughts and prayers of the nation tonight are with the passengers and crew of the snowbound crack streamliner Golden Gate Express.

"High in Raton Pass of the Rocky Mountains the ultra-modern diesel-electric train is stranded, a helpless victim of nature on a rampage. Temperatures of fifty to sixty degrees below zero prevail in the area.

"Sustained by packages of food and medicine that Air Force planes have dropped, every soul aboard must be waiting tensely as night closes in on the Rockies for the roar of snowplows which are working their way toward the train ..."

* * * *

The old gentleman in Drawing Room C said dreamily: "Zinnias, foxgloves and delphiniums." He was sitting up after a little nap and he sat up a trifle faster than he should have. A patch of his aorta the size of a fifty-cent piece blew out. He looked astonished as blood pumped into his chest cavity; for a moment there was considerable pain as the blood pressed against organs which had never been pressed before. The pain passed instantly, for the blood in his chest was blood that did not reach his brain. In swift succession the switches up there went open. Sight went, hearing went, kinaesthesia, the "muscle sense," went. He no longer felt alive and when his lungs and heart stopped he no longer was alive. Peristalsis continued in his bowels for a little while.

"Harvey?" asked his wife. "Aren't you well? Let me fix your pillow." She fixed his pillow. "The cold is dreadful," she said. "One would expect more consideration." She looked narrowly at her husband. No, she thought. He's had spells before. It can't be. Because it mustn't be, it can't be. "Perhaps the trip was a mistake," she said gaily. "When you've seen one great-grandchild you've seen them all. I'd far rather have spent the winter gardening even if California gardens never did seem quite real to me." He couldn't be—gone. It was not merely unlikely, it was impossible. He was wisely resting, that must be it, resting and conserving his strength. She noted that his trousers were wet and she almost tutted in vexation.

Naturally she would not mention such a thing, but as she chatted with Harvey she was also planning about this unfortunate new development. Really, it sometimes seemed old folks were never let off anything; now there was this business of—incontinence. She would have to persuade Harvey to wear a rubber device. You strapped them to your leg. And Harvey would pipe, when she delicately broached the subject, "Really unnecessary, my dear. Nothing the matter with me."

"Nothing the matter with you," she said to Harvey, "except false pride. I've had sixty years of it, starting with poor little Abbey when she got in trouble. She always was a little fool but she wouldn't have taken Lysol without that big thundering denunciation from you. For pity's sake, Harvey, she was my sister and all she wanted was a couple of hundred dollars so she could crawl away somewhere and have her baby. Do you feel like denouncing somebody now, Harvey? Why don't you?"

She began to cry. "It's over," she said. "It's over, and God forgive me, I'm so glad."

* * * *

Mrs. Groves was doing the grim tidying-up that has to be done after a death. Two deaths... The little conductor, no longer peppery, was writing out a report in the compartment with her. The girl had gone into delirium, remembered she was a believer or had been once, and taken Dr. Groves for a priest. The theology of it confused Mrs. Groves. Her husband had no power of absolution, so the girl, according to her lights, was now either in Hell or Purgatory. However, there was a recognized lay baptism, so the faithful would say the infant was now in Heaven instead of Limbo, which was probably just as well. Limbo was inhabited by unbaptized babies and such distinguished pagans as Aristotle and Averrhoes. They couldn't have much to say to each other. But could a follower of the heretical Luther administer a valid lay baptism, she wondered? And there was some sin they had called "exposing the sacrament to nullity." Perhaps Dr. Groves had done that and thereby damned himself. On the other hand there was the possibility under their own beliefs that he was already damned, not being one of the Elect. At this she snorted defiance to John Calvin; if theology stated that such a man as her husband could be eternally damned for no fault of his own, so much the worse for theology.

Somebody rapped respectfully on the door; the conductor put down his report and opened it. "Hello, Cutshaw," he said. It was a porter, a big man in a plaid overcoat.

"Excuse me, Mr. Simms," he said hesitantly. "I heard—I couldn't hardly believe it—"

The nurse drew back the sheet and Cutshaw looked at the small body. "Tan-color, all right," the porter said softly. "Poor little feller. Maybe better this way. Scuse me for disturbing you, miss." He slipped out quietly and the conductor locked the door and resumed working on the report.

"She still open?" he asked the nurse.

"No. After the infant died Dr. Groves sutured her."

"Then I guess that's all," he said. "You finished?"

"Yes." They went out and the conductor locked up from the outside. "First time on a train of mine with a mother and child both," he said. "Usually one or the other pulls through, if not both. But—considering—maybe Cutshaw was right."

* * * *

Officer Candidate Milton F. Martinson lay in a commandeered drawing room in the dark. It was a couple of hours since the tired-faced doctor had treated him, dressing his frozen toes and face. They blazed with pain. He should have remembered. Cold Weather Survival: "Below the freezing point every additional mile per hour of wind is physiologically equal to one degree lower temperature ..." Perhaps it had been twenty below and the wind had been blowing forty, equals sixty below. That was the way they froze meat, in big blast tunnels at zero degrees with a hundred-mile gale forced through them, equals a hundred below. He tried to grimace but choked with pain from his frozen face. Frozen meat.

They'd take off his toes, perhaps. It would be a great relief, both to end the pain and—the competition. From then on he'd be a cripple. His mother wouldn't nag him ever again to go out and play like the other kids; he'd be a cripple. He'd get a discharge, maybe the Soldier's Medal for risking his life in a civilian emergency. A limp and a little strip of enameled metal to wear in his lapel—people would come to certain conclusions and he wouldn't stop them.

No more competing, no more O.C.S., morning pushups, rope traverse, wall scaling that left him racked and gasping for an hour to the astonishment of the other candidates. Sleep as late as you want, get a little clerking job somewhere, read, watch television. Be the Man Who Has Had It...

Good-bye to O.C.S., thought the Man Who Had It. Sand tables, the school solution, Rifle Squad in the Attack, .75 mm. Recoilless Rifle Defensive Positions, Voice of Command, Company Administration, the Morning Report is the daily history of the company, your mortar section is cut off in this position with three days of fire your forward observer reports an enemy platoon with automatic weapons approaching from the north your ground phone line to Company has been cut you have an S.C.R. 400 but Battalion does not respond Mr. Martinson what do you do?

You yawn. Good-bye to all that.

In spite of the pain, he fell asleep comfortably out of the running for the first time in eighteen years.

* * * *

George had a hangover and Harold had a minor concussion. They sat side by side in the gathering dark of the day coach. It was noisy; a child was crying with the cold, two women were bickering loudly about a blanket and an old man was complaining to his grown and bad-tempered son.

"Dumb fool," George said, "letting him kick you that way. Should of grabbed his foot and stabbed him."

Harold held his head tenderly and shook it. "You're the dumb fool, George. Guy did me a favor, way I look at it. What if I'd of stabbed him, then what? He saved me from the Stebbins Temper, that's what he did. All us Stebbinses flare up and then we're sorry afterwards. Got an uncle in Stoney Hill Prison and he's never getting out unless he gets a pardon. He worked on the Road Force twenty years and then he got too feeble so they just stuck him in a cell. For what? The Stebbins Temper. He stabbed a man, no reason except his temper. Don't like to say it, George, but you're mistaken."

George digested it for a few minutes. "Maybe I spoke hastily," he said. And then after another pause: "Figure we'll get out of here all right?"

"We got out of worse places all right."

"God, yes… I've been thinking. I kind of wish I had a Bible now. Wish it was light enough to read it a little."

"I know lots of verses. From Sunday School. Won some prizes, matter of fact."

"No! You remember any?"

"Well, lemme see. There's: Take all that thou hast and give to the poor." He fell silent.

After a while George said: "Funny you should bring up that one. Think maybe we ought to do just that?"

It happened that they were reclining in moderate comfort despite the cold. From the plump traveling bags in the rack above their heads they had pulled out all manner of clothing, knitted skull caps and sheeplined Korea hats with ear flaps. Harold said evasively: "Hell, we're not rich. We just go to school."

George listened for a moment to the crying child and said miserably: "No use. You saying that verse was a Sign, Harold. We gotta do what's right."

Harold swore a little and then got up clumsily, shedding blanket and overcoat. He heaved down the suitcases, and emptied them. They were still grumbling when they stumbled down the dark aisle passing out the clothes where they seemed most needed.

They finally got to sleep, shivering, wrapped in a single blanket and with their feet and legs shoved into their suitcases.

* * * *

Cor chase my Aunt Fanny up a gum tree if he hasn't gone to sleep, thought the lieutenant's wife incredulously. Sleep! We're stuck on a snowbound train, it's unspeakably cold, we're just a little hungry, between my fur coat and the blankets we're just a little chilly—and he can sleep. Maybe it's something they learn at The Point. Spanish, Arabic, Civil Engineering and How to Fall Asleep Anywhere.

And he didn't even—well, I was a little snappish with him. I'll make it up to him in San Francisco. I'll be very sweet and tender and tears will tremble in my eyes when I see him off but they won't spill over so he can tell his new friends at the Officer's Club out there how swell I was, real Army all the way.

And in San Francisco I'll have to get in touch with this Yaeger man right away. Night clerk, Hotel Pharmacy, midnight to eight, Monday through Saturday, Mr. Yaeger, I'm Mrs. Clemens. Mrs. Vanhomrigh tells me you put up a remarkable skin lotion… And if he's on vacation or away sick or something?

Her heart began to pound at the thought. He wouldn't be, he couldn't be. But—there was this Larry who had done her a favor. He seemed to know things. He seemed to have connections. She'd have to keep in touch with him. She was awfully new at this business. Just barely old enough at it to know she couldn't get out of it…

The "remarkable skin lotion." It cost fifty dollars a bottle, which would hold her for a week—or would it? She wondered. Already she had taken three of the tablets when she had expected to take only one, but perhaps they were weak, diluted—no; not from a doctor's bag they weren't. So for two weeks in San Francisco she'd need one hundred dollars, which Thank God she had. It meant she'd spend the hundred on skin lotion instead of a few other things, like—like food and clothes. To Hell with buying your own food, she thought. That Larry, he would be glad to take her to dinner and gladder to stay for breakfast. She really would have to keep in touch with him; he seemed to be in funds. And when he left San Francisco a lady with her looks and figure and talent should have no trouble finding a replacement. The main thing was that she kept well ahead on her supply of—skin lotion. Perhaps if she had a thousand dollars she could buy twenty bottles. God, God, what a wonderful feeling that would be! To have twenty weeks' supply, not to have to even think about it for five whole months!

Just—when you want some, take some, in a civilized way without any hole-and-corner nonsense about it.

Where could she get a thousand dollars, she wondered? She had heard jokes about "hundred dollar girls" and once her husband had kindly explained that there weren't really any such thing. There were just girls, and they asked for as much as they thought they could get from a man, and sometimes it was twenty dollars, often probably a hundred. Maybe sometimes more, though he personally doubted it unless it was on one of those crazy business-entertainment expense-account things.

She felt tense, very tense. It was too foolish, lying there in the dark and chill when a good night's sleep lay within arm's length. Too foolish. She reached out to her handbag almost absent-mindedly, opened the catch one-handed, dipped in and fished out a pill. She swallowed it dry and waited for the mild glow to begin, which eventually it did. As she drifted off to sleep she drowsily wondered if it wouldn't be pleasant to feel that "ping" old Charlie had told her about, to feel it slam you like a sweet padded mallet into dreamland. Of course she wouldn't get sores or abscesses from a needle; she had deft, small hands and knew what she was doing...

CHAPTER XXXIV
THE COCKTAIL PARTY

Boyce and Foreman stood in the dark corridor outside Mona Greer's compartment. The wire service man snapped his cigarette lighter for a moment to check the number on the door. He saw the number, and two plumes of steam from their breaths. The corridor was murmurous with the sharp creak of contracting metal, distant clamor from the coaches, the scream of a faraway baby reverberating between the narrow walls.

The floor coverings salesman raised his hand to rap timidly twice, and between the first and second rap he prayed: Let it all be some kind of gag, just a crazy guess of Foreman's. Let it come out right somehow. She wants me and needs me, and nobody ever needed anybody the way I need her. Let it come out right. Let it not end in a dirty joke on her and me. "C-c-c-cold," he mumbled to Foreman.

Foreman waited, thinking: Anybody home? This is the Angel of Death calling, Miss Greer. The next voice you hear will be the executioner's. And then silently snorted at himself. It's a charade, he thought. Kill that creature? Why? Merely to keep her from perverting one more girl, merely to keep her from wrecking one more life? And he answered himself: Yes. That's why.

Inside the dim compartment Joan Lundberg said: "They seem to have arrived." Will they help me? But how absurd. I don't want to be—helped.

Mona smiled: "We'll feed them a couple of cocktails, sling the bums out and then ..." She took three dance steps to the door and flung it open. "Mr. Boyce! Come in—if you can see your way."

He blundered in.

"Hold the door," said Foreman's tight voice. "I'm here too."

"Then our little party's complete. My little Joan is the graceful shadow in the corner. Isn't this barbaric?"

Foreman asked: "Got a bottle of gin? Gin's best."

"Surely you're not going to gulp it from the bottle, Mr. Foreman?" she asked sweetly. "I know you newspapermen, but—"

Foreman said: "If you can bring yourself to sacrifice a bottle of gin, Miss Greer, I can provide light and a little heat."

She felt for the square-faced bottle in the traveling bar and passed it to him. "Work your alchemy," she commanded.

"No alchemy; just an old Army game. If there isn't a cord or anything like that, the next step is for me to take out a shoelace."

"Oh, a spirit lamp! Clever you! But I didn't know you had liquor to burn in the Army."

"Some of the black-market schnapps they peddled in Germany was a hell of a lot safer to burn than to drink. Good friend of mine went blind from a bottle of fourteen-year-old uebermensch swapped him for two packs of Luckies and a bar of K Ration chocolate. Always figured he got the worst of the deal. You got any string?"

"If you'll hold up my lighter, Mona," came Joan's composed voice, "I'll get my knitting. Would yarn be all right, Mr. Foreman?"

"Perfect. Best stuff next to a shoelace, and I don't feel like surrendering mine. Might have to step outside and I'd hate to throw a shoe out there."

Her lighter flared. She passed it to Mona, who held it high while Joan fumbled in a suitcase and produced a ball of baby-blue yarn. Foreman took it, snapped off a length and said thanks. He doubled and redoubled it and stuffed it into the neck of the square-faced bottle.

"Now, Mr. Foreman?" Mona Greer asked.

"Give it a moment to soak up. Now light it."

The lighter swooped down and the bulky wick caught, burning with an orange-tipped blue flame the size of a silver dollar. Like many a wrecked basement or Siegfried line pillbox Foreman had seen by similar light, the compartment came alive. The stage was set, the players in their places. Mona was a tragedy queen in fur robes, Joan an enchanted princess in blue, Boyce a comic dwarf yearning at her, and he—? The First Assassin?

"That's very pretty and very clever, Mr. Foreman," Mona said. "If you had money I'd marry you."

"Best offer I've had all week," he said. "You know what my last offer was?"

"Can't have been Babs Hutton," Mona said, cogitating. "She's married to that tennis-playing German."

"My last offer," said Foreman, "was to go to Frisco and do a job or wind up in the Chicago Drainage Canal with crabs eating my face."

Joan gasped; Boyce tried a nervous laugh and then said: "I don't get it," and waited for the joke to be explained.

"It's not essential that you get it," said Foreman. "I just wanted to indicate to those present that I'm in a peculiar line of work with its own standards."

"People 'bump people off' in your line of work?" Mona asked with amusement.

"Not as much as they used to, Miss Greer," he said, "but it's still a useful technique they occasionally resort to."

She shuddered elaborately and sat down beside Joan. She put her arm around her and said: "I'll protect you, darling." Joan laughed and said: "I'm not afraid. I thought there was something fishy about Mr. Foreman from the start."

"Ah—that's a very clever stunt with the gin," said Boyce, suffering on his face.

"Gin," said Mona, rising. "And my duties as a hostess are recalled to me. Since the gin is serving a nobler purpose, we shall have Manhattans."

Foreman said idly: "Thought you might have suggested Orange Blossoms, Bronxes, something like that." Old timers. Prohibition stuff. Get Miss Greer a little bit off balance. The first step toward murder. She had deliberately declined his hint; apparently the die was cast.

Her voice was a little cold: "You prefer such neolithic concoctions, Mr. Foreman? Perhaps I can mix you a Pisco Punch right out of the Gold Rush days?"

"I've heard they were lethal," he said. "A Manhattan would be satisfactory." Second warning, Miss Greer.

She reached for the Vermouth bottle in the portable bar.

"Dear old Manhattan," he said. "The old Brevoort, Richard Harding Davis, poor Bill Porter paralyzing himself on fifteen absinthe drops, the flaring gaslights and the rattling horse cars—those were the days, eh, Miss Greer?"

Even Boyce saw Mona's icy rage. She said calmly through it: "My young friend, I think you'd better leave. You don't seem inclined to be pleasant tonight and it's too cold to fence with a callow hack from a copydesk."

"Think you're man enough to put me out?" he asked.

"Mr. Foreman!" Joan snapped.

"By God—" Mona said hoarsely.

His face fell. "Gosh, I'm sorry," he said. "I thought you were kidding, Miss Greer, and I were only joking back. Did I say something wrong? I'm terribly sorry."

Mona Greer sat down and after a pause said: "You have a crude sense of humor, Foreman."

"Some people think I'm killingly funny." Third warning.

"To me," she said, "you are merely funny without qualification."

Bitch, this is where I take over. She was mixing the Manhattans. He blithely remarked: "The cocktails won't be what your guests have come to expect, Miss Greer. No ice."

Boyce laughed. "I won't mind," he said. He blew a plume of his breath into the little glow of the spirit lamp. "In fact you can warm mine up if you like."

Mona poured four glasses and handed them around.

"To the Chicago Drainage Canal," she said, looking Foreman full in the face.

They sipped. "God, that's good," said Joan.

"A little warm," Foreman said critically, "but good. Joan, your toast?"

She looked at the two men and said defiantly: "To Mona Greer, novelist, patriot, world traveler, friend of the working girl and crack bartender."

"That's not fair," said Mona, delighted. "I can't drink when the toast's to me."

"Sneak one," said Boyce miserably. "We won't look."

Feet shambled down the corridor outside. A little girl was squeaking that she din' wanna go outside, it was cold outside. Her mother grimly told her that they had gotta go outside for doo-doo, there wasn't no place in the train for it no more. The voices died.

"Down your hot toddy, Miss Greer," said Foreman, "while I think up a witty remark." She sipped. He announced: "To General Francis Sullivan, whose leadership of the great Northwest Expedition of 1779 broke the ridgepole of the Iriquois Longhouse and secured the Indian Frontier against a redcoat invasion from Canada." In an aside to Boyce he explained: "An ancestor of mine."

"Oh?" said Boyce. "Well, if ancestors are all right, I give you Matthew G. Boyce, born a farmer's son who rose to brakeman on the Erie and died in 1927 of T.B. leaving a mortgaged shack and eight hundred dollars in medical and funeral expenses to his loving family. Quite a boy, Pop was. A real Horatio Alger type, only nothing ever worked out quite right for him either."

They drained their glasses. Joan Lundberg was the last to raise hers and she drank slowly, not looking at the floor coverings man.

"Pour a second round, Foreman," said Mona Greer lazily. "I'm too comfortable next to my little Joan to move."

Foreman measured the rye, Vermouth and bitters into the pitcher. As he stirred he mourned: "Too bad—no ice."

"There's snow outside," Mona said, piqued.

That was it. That was murder. She was saying his lines now; the initiative was his.

He asked, showing nervousness: "What do you think, Boyce?"

Boyce said: "Ah—it's been used, the snow."

"Should be all right farther out," Foreman mused, exulting. "Some people were going way out when it was still light and collecting it to melt for drinking water."

"Mr. Foreman," Mona said with amusement, "you like it cold. You're the bartender; do your duty, go out and get us a pitcher of snow." She extended the drinking water pitcher that came with the compartment. Her face was regal in the flickering light.

"Sorry," he said, forcing a flush. "I'm a little nervous about charging out into the dark at fifty below, or whatever it is by now."

"He's right," Joan said unexpectedly. "It's much too dark. A person could get turned around out there and that would be that."

Foreman held his breath for a moment, but Mona spoke her line, not knowing that it had been forced on her like a magician's card—or why. With a look of infinitely amused scorn she drawled: "Very well. I'll go where—angels, would you say?—fear to tread."

"Hell," said Foreman, "I'll go. A drink's a drink."

Joan said: "This is nonsense. Nobody's going. It's fifty below or worse and the wind's terrible and the drinks are quite cold enough."

But of course Mona Greer had to follow through on a gesture... She was pulling on her dainty, fur-topped overshoes; she said derisively: "Mr. Foreman's worried about the wind and the cold, darling; I'm not."

"Mona," Joan protested weakly. "At least take this." She handed her the ball of yarn.

"How sweet. Shall I knit an afghan with it, darling?"

"No. Tie it to the steps or something. I mean it. It's pitch-black out there."

Mona said: "And unreel it like a spider as I wander into the wintry wastes, or like Ariadne leaving a clue for bold Theseus. All right, darling, and thank you."

Foreman felt the knife in his pocket. He had envisioned following the creature into the dark, perhaps striking her—and knew he couldn't do it. This way was much the better way. "I'll go along as anchor man," he said.

"You will be quite superfluous."

"As usual. But why not?"

"Come along, then. You can't do any harm," she said. A smiling slap in the face.

Holding her cigarette lighter up before them, she led Foreman down the aisle to the vestibule. "Here," she said, handing him the pitcher and the lighter. The lighter was beginning to burn blue.

In the flickering glow she knotted an end of the yarn very firmly to one of the vestibule grabirons and opened the train door. Had they thought it was cold inside? The cold rolled in and clutched them like an iron hand. She gasped as it seized her chest. She said softly: "I wonder if this is really—"

Foreman laughed amiably.

She snatched the pitcher and lighter from him in a rage and swiftly climbed down the steps, unrolling the yarn behind her. With his hand on the yarn and his eyes straining into the blackness he sensed that she was being very careful indeed. Mona Greer was not risking her life; not the life that might bring her so many more little blonde twists to corrupt and so many well-meaning young men to make fools of.

He saw out there a tiny spark of blue: the lighter. It dipped; she must be inspecting the snow for purity. The yarn tightened and slackened under his fingers; she was trying farther out again. Again the minute spark. This time it would be all right. She would scoop a pitcher-full of snow, feel her way carefully back along the yarn through the blackness to the blackness that was the train, climb the steps, flushed and triumphant—

You can't do any harm.

He whipped out the knife. Snick. And cut the yarn.

He noticed numbly that his ears were ringing with the cold.

Now she must be feeling the yarn, finding it loose, surprisingly loose, and now she must be noticing that she's not feeling her way back along it but winding it up slackly.

"Foreman!" came a sharp call from the darkness, with the silvery voice not edged by alarm. She couldn't be more than fifty feet away, and only bravado had taken her out that far.

"Foreman!"

Now she must be standing there in the dark feeling the beginning of panic. Go this way? Or that way? Or stand still and wait for an answering shout from the ineffectual heavy who had tried to spoil her little game with the little blonde twist?

"Foreman! Can—can anybody hear me?"

No, Mona. Not in the train with blankets pinned to the windows. If you'd gone out the other side then you would have seen your own compartment's window brightly lit with the flame of your own gin, but that was the gentlemen's side and you were a perfect lady.

"Foreman! Anybody! Can anybody hear me?" Her voice broke. Now she must be telling herself that she would have to move, that she couldn't just stand there and freeze. Now she must be telling herself that she couldn't miss the train, that surely she just had to walk straight forward in a straight line and she'd hit the train or if she were terribly, unthinkably off her course she'd hit the tracks and just follow them to the train.

"Can anybody hear me?" The voice was hoarse with panic—and more distant. Now she must be trudging on, sure that she would blunder into the steel cars at the next step or two, feeling ahead of herself with her hands so she wouldn't bump her face—

"Fore-ma-a-an!" It was the distant wail of a soul in Hell. Now the cold must be getting to her; they said it was forty below. Now she must be floundering in snowdrifts she knew should not be there.

A choked animal howl without words sounded faintly in his numb ears. And still he waited. Forty below.

A long minute later there was a howl that was less than animal, surely the last vestige of her life. And still he waited.

There was no further sound. There was only the desolate blackness and the still cold like a vice clamped on his chest.

Abruptly he closed the train door and went through the vestibule into the stench of the darkened car and the night-noises; whimpering; groans; curses. His feet were like wooden clogs.

A figure loomed before him: Boyce.

"Where's Miss—" Boyce began, and then broke off. His eyes were riveted to Foreman's gloved right hand. Foreman still clutched the open knife.

In a dry, hoarse voice he hardly recognized as his own, Foreman said: "I killed her. I cut the cord and she froze. It's forty below out there."

"Shut up!" Boyce whispered. "Don't talk like that." He pried the knife from Foreman's hand and closed it and put it in his own pocket. "It could have been an accident—it was an accident. It broke by itself. You didn't kill her!"

There was a long pause. "You're right, of course," Foreman said.

He watched as Boyce went to the door that leaked light around its end and opened it. In the brief moment he saw Joan's face by the light of the spirit lamp, puzzled and expectant. And the door closed.

Foreman walked to his own compartment past the groans and snores and crying children, swearing adults, the coughs and snorts and curses in the dark. His foot burned with cold and it was dark, but he found his way without stumbling.

With a tumbler of whisky in his hand he thought: Civil murder. I've done it and there's no undoing it. Now there's only one other thing to do and that's to get myself executed for murder. I have a feeling that I could execute myself the way poor Mike did, with this bottle and a few thousand more like it. A messy and undignified way to die, and it takes twenty years and sometimes more. Or like the red-head I could take to drugs, which is quicker but not quick enough.

I can't live with this. It was a silent scream. Greer's face, Greer's voice—he had ended them, turned them off. Am I sorry? I don't know. What I know is that I can't live with it.

There must be a way out of it. Out of living with the face and voice of Greer, out of the slime I've tumbled into. And he knew suddenly that there was a way. First he would have to make the contact in San Francisco. Then he would have to develop it and do at least half the job. Then he would have to buy a tape recorder. And then soon, quite soon, he would be out of it. And everything.

A distant roar shivered through the train as something crashed into it at 4:45 A.M.

Boyce woke with a start. Beside him Joan was crying softly. The spirit lamp had burned dry and gone out, with a curl of smoke from the charred wick.

"Joan," he said, looking at her wonderingly.

"Don't misunderstand," she said, blinking away tears. "It's stopped hurting. Anyway, I didn't mind." She clung to him. "Was I crazy? Hypnotized? By her?"

"You were scared and running," he said. "But now you know there's nothing to be scared of."

"Now I know," she said softly. She thought of her father. The face wasn't demoniacal at all any more. The beard wasn't mephistophelian; it was simply a little beard as worn by a rather sad little man who had been running hard too. His crackling, bitter voice? She heard it now in her ears, but with new overtones of tiredness and gentle humor to which she had been deaf for too long. She hated him no more.

"This is real," she said slowly. "Not like it would have been with—"

"—a certain unhappy woman," he finished. "This is real, darling; you're stuck with me. For better or worse, for richer or poorer. And it's going to be for poorer, I guess. She'll get one of those damn Illinois divorces. Stick the knife into me and twist it for maybe two hundred a month."

"You'd be cheap at twice the price," she said, and kissed him.

The train shivered again.

"We'd better get out of here," Boyce said, leaping from the berth. He groped for a match and struck it, began to struggle into his clothes. "Get dressed, Joan. Or we'll have some explaining to do."

She whipped her own clothes on. Her nerves overcame her at the door and she clutched at him. "Is she really—gone?"

"Gone like a nightmare in the morning," he said grimly.

"Yes," she said. "A nightmare. One of those running-in-glue nightmares." She hugged him and said: "It's good to be awake again."

They stepped carefully down the aisle and clutched each other as the train jolted and crashed. The car was a smelly bedlam of excited and hilarious passengers. Hoarded matches were being recklessly struck; people were shaking hands and laughing.

"Our seat," said Boyce. He poked the rump of a woman who was sprawled over both halves of it. "This is ours," he told her as she shook herself blearily in the light of the match he held. She got up wordlessly and shambled off, stretching in the cold.

The lights began to glow dimly! A crazy, happy cheer crashed through the car; Boyce and Joan sat very close together.

Somebody—it was the tall trainman—yelled from the forward end of the car: "Can I have yer attention please? Snowplows and an axillery engine have reached us. We'll have light and heat up to normal soon. We'll have samwiches and coffee passed out to your seats soon. There's a doctor up front. Anybody needs treatment, please go up front. We oughta be in Phoenix by noon."

He passed hurriedly down the aisle. The conductor followed him, brisk and peppery again, snapping at questioning passengers: "Not now. Gotta get things organized again."

"The hell with San Francisco," Boyce said. "Let's get off at Phoenix."

"What a wonderful—"

She fell silent as Foreman walked slowly down the aisle. He stopped and said to them: "Think I'll find that doctor up front. I seem to have a touch of frostbite. You two all right?"

"Yes," said Joan impulsively. "Everything's wonderful."

"Wonderful," he said woodenly, and stumped down the aisle.

Bless you, my children, he thought. The price will be high, but from your eyes I think it was worth the price I must pay.

Pilar Mackenzie y del Torres and her child lay cold and uncaring.

Dr. and Mrs. Groves rested at last, fallen asleep slumped over their bed in the middle of their prayers.

And outside in the dark a wolf fed on another wolf.